SLIGGERS

MICHAEL YOWELL

SEVERED PRESS
HOBART TASMANIA

SLIGGERS

ISBN: 978-1-925840-11-7

AUTHOR'S NOTE

I have always loved the ocean. The idea of a separate, different world containing a myriad of unique life forms is fascinating. Since man's early exploration across the seas, tales of sea monsters have surfaced. These were undoubtedly inspired by the strange creatures men witnessed for the first time during their travels on the water. Whether they were narwhals, oarfish, hammerhead sharks, or giant squid, they were extraordinary and frightening.

And there are still creatures living in the murky depths that we haven't even seen yet. Who's to say there aren't actual monsters down there in the deep?

...Or closer to shore?

This book is dedicated to everyone who still has a spark of fearful imagination regarding the ocean.

PROLOGUE

The cove was calm tonight, as usual. Warm easterly winds pulled waves inland from the Atlantic, but the heaving swells broke upon contact with the reef and dissipated quietly into the water of the deep cove beyond. There would be good fishing in the still water.

Looking up at the full moon, Earl Goates grunted his approval. The moonlight in the clear sky would make fishing easier for him. He would be able to see his gear without having to use his flashlight. That meant less attention drawn to him from the keen eyes of the fish below.

With a six-pack of cold beer in hand, Earl locked the back door of his two-bedroom house and crossed the weathered porch to gather his fishing gear. After depositing the beer safely inside a Styrofoam cooler, he lugged his pole, tackle box, and cooler from the back porch to the eight-foot dinghy he kept tied at the edge of the cove.

The boat was a rickety old thing, worked over by many years of sunlight, salt water, and sand. But it, like his small house on the beach, was left to Earl when his father died, so it was a cherished belonging. And he loved night fishing in that boat as much as his father did.

The sixty-year-old fisherman set his gear inside the dinghy, untied the rope, and sat down inside. Then he shoved off with one oar until the water accepted his boat and carried him out. Gripping the second oar, he paddled into the sizable cove.

He stopped when he reached the center of the cove. Surrounded by an amphitheater of rock wall, the waters of Pirate's Bend were quiet. Plenty of good fish had been pulled out of this cove over the years. It was an ideal feeding ground for young gray snapper and other shallow water fish. Earl opened a beer from the cooler, took a few chugs while admiring the moon's soft reflection on the water, then began to bait his hook.

A heavy splash was heard from the far end of the cove, echoing across the dark water. Earl's ears perked. That was definitely something swimming in the cove, breaking just off the shore. Might be a large redfish, might be a sandbar shark, but either way it would be a worthy catch. If he could hook and land whatever it was, he'd be able to find a buyer for it tomorrow morning. With a smooth but motivated stroke, Earl rowed his dinghy toward the area of the splash.

Following the reflection of moonlight on the water, he pulled his way across Pirate's Bend until he was about twenty feet from the rocky shore. There he stopped and listened.

Another hearty splash interrupted the quiet, this time coming from a tight notch of the cove on Earl's left side. Grinning, he slowly rowed the boat in the direction of the splash.

When he arrived at the spot, an eerie silence greeted him. The rock walls surrounding the ten-foot-wide notch blocked out the sounds of the nearby ocean, making it surprisingly quiet where Earl now was. He carefully set down his oars and prepared to drop his line just over the side.

A lazy lapping of water was audible as something barely breached the surface behind him. He whipped his head around to see the ripples it left behind, and he immediately noticed the invasive stench of rotten eggs. He frowned.

Suddenly he heard – and felt – scratching, coming from the underside of the wooden boat. Something was vigorously investigating the bottom of the hull, the scratching growing louder and more intense. *An aggressive shark?* he feared. Eyes wide, Earl dropped his pole and gripped both sides of the dinghy.

The water erupted behind him. As he was turning his head, Earl felt something cold wrap itself around him and pierce his body, penetrating deep through his clothing into his muscle tissue. The sulfuric stench returned, then disappeared when he was pulled over the side and chilly sea water rushed into his nostrils and mouth. He felt something digging and tearing into him, sensed the warmth of his own blood in the water around him, and then he was gone.

Minutes later, the water had settled to once again hold the still reflection of the moon.

CHAPTER 1

The funeral was every bit as heartrending as expected. The community had lost a dear old friend in Mabel Parker, and the service drove that bitter fact home even deeper. After the reverend concluded the service, the townspeople in attendance followed her son out back to the church's limestone patio to offer their condolences.

Mason Parker had just returned home after graduating college. At the spry age of twenty-two, he had planned to figure out the rest of his life while staying with his mother for the summer. He had only been home for a few days when she died in her sleep Monday night.

Mason had found Mabel in her bed the next morning, looking peaceful as could be. When he tried to wake her, her skin was cold and lifeless. After ten minutes of staring at her in shock, he gathered himself and called the police station. His memory of that day was all but a blur of cold skin, shaky hands, dealing with the sheriff and coroner, and ultimately locking himself inside a quiet house that enveloped his sobs and sighs.

The service was held at Mabel's church, naturally, where all her friends and clergy gathered to remember her. Reverend Jenkins delivered the memorial with just the right blend of sorrow, faith, and humor. But in the end, everybody was still devastated by the loss of their beloved friend Mabel. And now they were on the back patio, comforting her son and each other.

Mason only owned one suit, which he wore today to honor his mother. Mabel's friends commented on how handsome he looked in that navy blue suit, but to him it felt like a straitjacket. It was uncomfortable, constricting, and burning him up. The muggy summer heat under a South Carolina sun made sure of it.

He removed his jacket and draped it over his arm. Sweat stains were visible on his shirt, but he no longer cared. It was just too damn hot to keep the jacket on. Plus, the gathering around him was beginning to make him feel a bit confined as well.

With a polite, belabored smile, Mason continued to respond kindly to all those who expressed their genuine grief and sympathy. They were sweet people, a good group of folk that were part of what gave this small seaside town of Sweetboro its unique charm. Sure, there were people in town that were less than desirable, as in any town, but everybody that came for the funeral today was someone Mason knew and liked.

Sweetboro was tucked away in a small bay along the Atlantic coastline. With no major highways anywhere nearby, the town had managed to retain its quaint, tight-knit identity. There was some tourism – mostly people that were looking for a quiet, uncrowded beach – but for the most part the town's economic survival was self-sustaining. Sweetboro consisted of two grocery stores, two banks, three churches, schools, a single gas and auto repair shop, a small hospital, a police station, a post office, several shops, restaurants, and a dock mooring half a dozen fishing boats.

Main Street ran from the dock inland, through the center of town, and to the state highway far beyond. In the outlying hills on either side of town, nestled throughout the oaks and pines, were the family homes of the town's residents. Sweetboro was a simple yet charming town.

Mason's family had lived here for four generations. He had been raised a proper, God-fearing Southern boy by a doting but disciplining mother. Mabel had to do it on her own, since Mason's father died in a car accident when Mason was just a toddler. But the community had rallied to her, offering all their support.

Mabel's best friend Sherrie Robinson, who owned a restaurant near the dock, was the most helpful. Sherrie, another widow, spent much time at the Parker house. As a result, her daughter and Mason became best friends. Her name was Beverly, but for some reason she took to the shortened variant Eaver (due in part to how she pronounced her own name as a baby). Mason and Eaver were soon inseparable. The two kids spent practically all their waking hours together, whether they were climbing trees, fishing, or playing on the beach, and their time together made it easier for Mabel to continue serving the community as their mail carrier.

Mason had spotted Sherrie and Eaver earlier during the service. He was glad they came. It brought him a sense of family. Now, on the back patio of the church, he saw them mingling with the rest of the congregation.

Then he saw Sheriff Steele, on duty and in uniform, which surprised him a little. Jimmy Steele knew everybody in town, including Mabel, so he undoubtedly took time away from work to attend her service here. The sheriff made eye contact with Mason, and he made his way across the patio to the young man.

Holding his hat against his chest, a solemn frown formed beneath his bushy, brown mustache. "I'm so sorry about your ma. How ya holdin' up, Mason?"

"As good as I can," Mason shrugged. "I still can't believe she's gone. I go numb just thinking about it."

"I know, son, I know. Your ma was a great lady, and a great friend. We're all gonna miss her somethin' fierce. But we can take comfort knowing she's with the Lord now." The sheriff rested a hand on Mason's shoulder. "She was awful proud of you, though, I do know that. Used to talk up a storm about you when you were away to college. You made her real happy, Mason."

Mason felt tears welling in his eyes, and he fought to control them. "Thank you, Sheriff Steele, I appreciate that." He took a deep breath. "All I've ever wanted was to make her proud."

"She'll be looking in on you from up there, don't you worry. I'm sure you'll always make her proud."

He switched to a more positive tone. "So you all done with college?"

"Yes sir."

"I heard you were studying criminal justice?"

The graduate nodded. "Bachelor of Science. I just need to decide exactly what area to work in. You know, crime scene investigation, criminal investigation, maybe juvenile justice."

"Well," said the sheriff, "I might be able to take on a good employee at the station."

Mason smiled. "You never know, Sheriff. Thanks."

The moment was interrupted by the vibrating of Steele's phone. It was Deputy Riggins calling. "Excuse me, son." The sheriff patted Mason's shoulder, then stepped aside to pick up the call from his deputy. "This is Steele, what's up?"

Curious, Mason listened in to the sheriff's side of the conversation.

"You sure it's blood? ...You think it's ol' Earl's? ...Pirate's Bend? ...Looks pretty bad, huh? ...Okay, Spud, I'm on my way. Keep it as intact as you can."

The sheriff ended the call and dutifully returned his hat to his head. Mason watched him walk briskly through the crowd, tip his hat to Sherrie and Eaver as he passed by, and disappear into the church to get to his car out front.

Eaver caught Mason's gaze and noticed that he was no longer talking to anybody else. She excused herself from her mother and approached her long-time friend. Mason could not help but notice the dress she was wearing. Eaver had chosen a dark purple summer dress for the somber occasion, so dark that it looked almost black in the shade. It was tasteful enough for a funeral, but also very enticing. It lay well on her slender figure.

She opened her arms and embraced him in a strong hug. "Hey, Mason. I'm so sorry... she was like a second momma to me."

"I know, Eaver. She loved you too." He released his hug and held her at arm's length. "You changed your hair."

"Just added highlights so it's not so dark." Her dark brown hair contained subtle streaks of highlighting, blending smoothly so that it all looked like one brighter tone. "And let it grow out a little longer. You like it?"

He did. Particularly the way the sunlight brought out the lighter shades. He was finding his childhood friend more attractive each year. "You look lovely, Miss Eaver."

She blushed a bit. "Thank you, sir. So do you. All handsome in that suit." She could not deny that he looked good; tall, slim, and cute, with wavy red hair that looked sharp against the navy blue clothing.

"Yeah, well I can't wait to get it off and get back in my shorts and tee. Just have to tough it out until I'm done here."

"Going straight back to the house after?"

"Yeah, some of the folks said they'd be by later with food and such."

"Are you going to stay there? I mean, even after... this?"

Mason nodded. "Sure, it's still my home. Guess it's mine literally, now. I deal with the lawyer on Monday and figure out all the legalities."

"I'm glad you'll be staying there. I've missed hanging out with you while you were away."

Being back in his hometown did bring a sense of solace over him, despite his recent loss. "I think I missed being home. It's not gonna be the same anymore, but I'm still glad I'm here."

"Maybe we can drive up to the Gardens sometime and paddle a canoe through the swamp, like we did when we were kids." She touched his shoulder gently. "Might do you good," she added with the sweetest Southern drawl.

He forced a smile through his sorrow. "Thanks, Eaver. That does sound nice."

"Are you gonna be okay tonight? Me and Momma could come over later if you like."

"No, thank you, I'll be fine." He knew it was a lie; he felt utterly alone and depressed. But it had always been his nature not to impose on anybody else. He was sure that he was strong enough to get through this. "No need for y'all to fret over me."

"Alright, sugar. But you just call on us if you need anything, okay?"

"Okay," he said. Then he watched while Eaver turned and walked away to find her mother among the crowd. *What a good friend*, he thought. She had always been there for him, ever since childhood.

At that moment he thought about the empty house waiting for him, and a pain shot through him. He realized he was not strong enough after all.

"Hey, Eaver?" he called, and she stopped. "On second thought, if you don't mind, I think I'd appreciate the company."

She nodded proudly. "We'll leave Cinch to close up the restaurant for us. See you around seven?"

"I'll be there. And thank you."

"No trouble a'tall, Mason. I'll go tell Momma."

CHAPTER 2

Jimmy Steele always felt uncomfortable at Pirate's Bend. There was something about the cove that made the sheriff feel cold and edgy. It had a dark aura about it, almost evil.

He had reservations about the cove ever since the tragedy. When he was a high school senior, he and his friends would drive there at night to drink beer and let loose. One particular June evening, when Jimmy wanted to go to a house party to do something different, his buddies still insisted on their usual routine of climbing down the cove face to build a fire by the water.

They had managed to coax two girls from school to join them, with the promise of supplying whatever alcohol they wanted, which made Jimmy feel a little better about missing the house party. Especially since one of the girls was somebody he had a secret crush on.

Her name was Samantha Kramer. A sweet but fairly quiet girl, she did not go out for sports, cheerleading, or any of the school clubs. But she was friendly enough – and pretty enough behind her glasses – to be socially included by her more popular classmates. Jimmy sat directly behind her in Social Studies class, and he spent more time admiring her thin waist and soft, pale neck than listening to the droning of his teacher.

She and her sister Amy were happy to be carousing with the boys tonight. A campfire at the water's edge would be more exciting than hanging out with the girls in town. Boys and alcohol would be a fun, refreshing change from their usual Friday night.

Once the group got to Pirate's Bend, they navigated down the rocks with their firewood and booze. Before long, they had built a lively campfire near the shoreline. And it did not take long for the alcohol they consumed to take effect on their inhibitions.

Samantha and Amy dared each other to dive into the dark seawater from one of the rocks. Naturally the boys encouraged this idea, figuring the girls would strip down to their bras and panties before getting wet. To the boys' delight, the sisters did peel their clothing to expose their underwear and smooth, willowy bodies.

Samantha was the first to scamper up the rocks to a decent ledge. She asked the others what dive she should attempt, and they gave their suggestions. Jimmy wanted to see a can opener, and that was what she decided to do. She took a step back, lunged forward off the ledge, and tucked a knee to her chest as she entered the water. The high splash erupted, then rained back down into the settling wake.

Jimmy smiled while waiting for her to resurface. The seconds continued to tick away, and Samantha still had not returned to the surface. Jimmy's smile slowly shrank into a tight frown. After half a minute, fear and panic set in.

He grabbed the flashlight and aimed its beam where Samantha had entered. It was hard to see through the turbidity of the water, but he briefly saw a glimpse of her white face, several feet below the surface. The image was something that would haunt him forever; her eyes wide in terror, her mouth screaming unheard. Then the currents brought in more sediment, erasing her from sight.

Jimmy and one of the other boys jumped in and swam to her in a vain attempt to rescue her. But when they were able to locate her limp arms in the darkness, they were unable to pull her up to the surface. It felt like the cove was pulling back. Finally, after many maddening failed attempts, they surrendered and returned to shore.

When the police arrived, no charges were filed. The teens were scolded for underage drinking and their parents were called to collect them, but the unfortunate death was deemed accidental. A diver was able to retrieve Samantha's body, after wresting her leg free from the two rocks it was jammed between. The diver determined she had gotten her ankle stuck in the rocks when she jumped into the water.

For years Jimmy stayed away from Pirate's Bend. It was a constant reminder of that tragic night. He finished high school without another visit to the cove.

That was not the only tragedy in Pirate's Bend. Shortly after Jimmy and his friends graduated, a young man was free-diving in the cove. Apparently he got lost or trapped in one of the underwater caves at the deepest end. His body was not found until a month later when divers finally found his corpse suspended in one of the many tiny, dark chambers in the caves.

Now that Jimmy was the town sheriff, it bothered him that the cove still had the effect it did on him. Despite his position of power, he still felt like a nervous kid at Pirate's Bend. A chill danced up his neck as the dirt road brought him along the edge of the cove. Seeing his deputy at the scene when he arrived made him feel a little better.

Deputy Carl Riggins grew up in Sweetboro, just as the sheriff did. Like many families in the town, his had remained in the family home for generations. He was thrilled to find a job as respectable as a policeman; there was not much other work in town that he would be happy doing. And the sheriff, having known Carl from high school, was glad to have Deputy Carl Riggins – whom he affectionately referred to as Spud – on the team.

"Whaddawe have here, Spud?" Sheriff Steele said while stepping out of the squad car.

"Looks like an animal attack of some kind," the deputy replied. "Lots of damage, and some blood spatter on the boat."

"Alright, let's get down there and take a look-see."

Deputy Riggins led his boss down the rocky slope to the water's edge. Gingerly, the sheriff followed to where the boat had washed up. The lifeless dinghy lay halfway in the water, capsized, showing deep scratches on most of the hull.

"Jesus," the sheriff muttered. "What coulda done *this?*"

"You got me, Sheriff. Look down on the side, you can see the blood."

"Yessir, I see it." Sheriff Steele reached down and gripped the edge, then pulled the boat over to expose the topside. As he expected, there was more spatter inside. "Hmm. That doesn't look good."

"No it doesn't. And I know ol' Earl, he was an excellent boatsman and swimmer. I checked his house, of course, but he's nowhere to be seen. And I know for sure this is his dinghy." He drew a deep sigh. "I think something got him."

The sheriff heaved the boat back over to inspect the hull again. "Something big, based on all the damage done to the underside. What's this?" The sheriff had noticed something, and the deputy followed his eyes to an object embedded in the hull.

"Is that a *tooth?*"

Sheriff Steele loosened the object from the wood and held it close to his face. It definitely looked like a tooth of some sort – long, thin, needle-like, dingy white. "Kinda looks like a tooth of a big sand tiger shark."

"Yeah, but you wouldn't find anything like that in these shallows." Deputy Riggins paused to contemplate. "Or would you?"

"No," the sheriff concurred. "Not somewhere like in here. But what else could this thing be from?"

"Bull sharks would swim in water like this."

"True, but their teeth are a lot different than this."

"Gators?"

The sheriff shifted his stance. "Shit, Spud. It's possible, but you know as well as I that gators tend to hide from men, not attack 'em." He spat into the foam on the rocky shoreline. "I got no idea what could've done this."

It's just Pirate's Bend, he told himself. *It takes life when it feels the need, no reasons or explanations.*

"I dunno, either. I suppose we could find an expert to tell us what it is."

"True." He handed the suspected tooth to his deputy. "Here, bag it and we'll bring it in with the rest." The sheriff glanced out across the water of the calm cove. "In the meantime, we got a missing person. Did you check the whole shoreline for a body?"

"Yessir, as soon as I recognized the boat."

"Alrighty then. Guess I better call out the diver."

Sheriff Steele climbed the hill back to his car, where he used his radio to call the station. The diver arrived shortly afterward, and the sheriff brought him down to the shore. Then the diver entered the brackish water and began his search for a body.

CHAPTER 3

Eaver and her mother arrived at the Parker house just as the last of the visitors were leaving the wake. Nodding to the departing neighbors as they passed by, the women climbed the six steps to the wrap-around porch of Mabel's country cottage. The modest house was a powder blue Colonial with white trim. The blue siding appeared faded and washed out this evening, but it was still a soft, welcoming shade.

Gripping a bag of barbeque with one hand, Sherrie rapped lightly on the front door. Eaver pulled her dress tight while waiting for Mason to appear. When he opened the door, he looked as downtrodden as he had during the funeral. Eaver's heart sank when she saw his eyes.

"Evening, ladies," he sighed. "Thanks for coming over. Please, come in."

"Hello, sweetie," said Sherrie, hugging him with her free arm. "We brought you over some good fixin's. Cinch even pulled the best parts of the pork for you and put a special sauce on the side."

Mason was not hungry, but he smiled anyway. "Mmm, he's always been the best cook in the county, far as I'm concerned. I'm glad he's still working for you."

"Yep, that ol' Louisiana Creole was an angel dropped at my doorstep. He's family, he is."

Mason led them inside to the dining room, where Sherrie set the barbeque on the table next to all the other food collected there. The townsfolk that had stopped by throughout the day had left a plethora of food, including cakes, pies, breads, casseroles, and a meatloaf from the owner of the larger grocery store. Mason would have enough food to last for weeks.

Eaver had also brought a bag, from which she pulled a bottle of Johnny Walker Black. "Mason, go fetch us some glasses for this."

He grimaced. "I'm not really in the mood for…"

"Hush it," said Sherrie, "and go get those glasses. This is exactly what you need right now."

Shrugging, Mason complied. He went to the kitchen and returned with three water glasses. He set them down between the abundant flowers and sympathy cards, and Eaver poured two fingers of whiskey in each glass.

"Shoot it down," Sherrie directed, and they did. "Feel better?" she asked. Mason winced, then nodded. Sherrie motioned for her daughter to pour another round.

Handing everyone their drinks, Eaver wrapped her arm inside Mason's and pulled him away from the dining table. "C'mon, let's sit a spell and talk."

When the three were situated on the patterned living room sofa, Sherrie began by taking Mason's hand in her own. "Your momma was a great friend, you know that?"

"Of course," he replied with a bittersweet smile. "You two were like sisters when I was growing up."

"And you know how happy you made her? Watching you grow up brought a light to her eyes. Why, I'm sure she's with us right now, smiling down at her son, the college boy! She's so damn proud of you."

Wiping the tears that were beginning to well, Mason nodded. "I hope you're right, Sherrie."

"I am. Now you make good on everything she taught and gave you, and make a great life for yourself. That's what she would've wanted."

"Hell, I'm not sure what I'm gonna do next. I wasn't planning on having to figure out my life until after the summer."

"Some people never figure that out," said Sherrie, "but you won't be one of them. Just be patient for now, you'll know soon enough what you want to do."

Mason shifted the focus to his friend. "What about you, Eave? Are you going to the community college?"

She dropped her head. "No, not yet. I don't have time, what with helpin' Momma run the restaurant."

Mason nodded. He practically grew up in Sherrie's Shack, at least for a few hours a day on his way home from school. Sherrie's Shack had been successful for many years, thanks to the masterful cooking skills of Sherrie and her cook Cinch. They served fantastic fried chicken, shrimp and grits, gumbo, and chowder; but their barbeque was the town favorite.

"But you love workin' for your Momma, Baby," toyed Sherrie.

Eaver rolled her eyes. "Yeah, 'cause *that's* what I want to do for the rest of my life." She refilled the glasses with more whiskey.

"It could be worse, you know. I'll retire someday, and the restaurant will be yours. And someday your kids'." Sherrie picked up her glass and began to drink.

"We'll see," was all Eaver could say.

"If you end up running the restaurant," Mason said, "just go easy on the ketchup."

Sherrie almost spit up her whiskey laughing. "Oh my Lord, you got that right, Mason! She's terrible about that."

"You still love your crab cakes and ketchup?" he asked, having always been astounded by her obsession with dousing crab cakes in ketchup.

Eaver nodded emphatically. "Hell yeah, the redder the better!"

"She ruins perfectly good crab cakes," mumbled Sherrie. "A crying shame." She finished her drink, and the others did the same. Eaver poured once more.

Sherrie redirected the conversation. "So how was college, sweetie?"

"Pretty good," Mason said. "Four years was a long time, lots of stress, but there were some good times mixed in there. I'm glad it's all finally over, though. Now if I can just figure out what type of job I want to get."

"And if you don't, you can work with Eaver and me at the restaurant."

He was quick with a response. "No ma'am, you wouldn't want *me* cooking anything."

Sherrie giggled. "Just teasin', sweetie. I'm sure you'll find something good. You're young, ambitious, smart, and have the world at your doorstep." She had no doubts that he would do well. "I swear you grew a few more inches in college," she added. "What are you now, like six-foot-two?"

Mason shrugged. "Sounds about right."

"Well, you look great," Sherrie praised. "You're a handsome young man."

He chuckled, motioning to her glass. "Then you must be getting a little buzzed, Miss Sherrie!"

She shooed the air. "Hush, you know you're handsome. Bet you had to beat the college girls off with a stick."

Looking at Eaver, he said, "That wasn't the case."

Eaver simply smiled. Mason had always been cute, in a plain way, but now he was a fine-looking young man. What used to be a goofy kid and best friend was now something more – someone she could become attracted to. Perhaps it was the whiskey.

She poured another shot.

The group spent some time reminiscing about Mason's mother, telling amusing stories and recalling some of the memorable moments of her life. It brought some peace to Mason, and he began accepting the finality of her death. After honoring her life with anecdotes and memories, Eaver decided it was time to liven up the mood a bit.

"Let's spend the day doing something fun tomorrow!" she offered, slapping an enthusiastic palm on Mason's thigh. "What would you like to do?"

Mason grinned, knowing his response would meet opposition. "Like rock climbing?"

Eaver shook her head. Mason had always loved scaling rocks and cliffsides, but she was scared to death of it. "No, Captain Spelunker, try again."

He laughed. "Alright, alright… no rock climbing."

"What do you say we go fishing? We could go get Danny and use his boat."

The idea was appealing to Mason. He had not seen Danny Young since high school. And Danny had a great little rowboat tied up behind his dad's house.

"How is Danny? Anything new with him?"

"Naw, not really. Still living with his dad, going to the community college, and trying to find work on the side. I don't think he's had anything stable since graduating high school."

"I always liked Danny. He was a good egg. It'll be fun to hang out with him tomorrow."

"I'll give him a call in the morning and we'll head over. He won't have any other plans, I'm sure."

"He still courtin' that Hannah girl?"

Eaver rolled her eyes. "He's trying, bless his heart."

Mason frowned. "What's the matter, she not all that sweet on him?"

"Not on *him*, but maybe his…"

Sherrie cleared her throat, stopping Eaver's speech. "Now, gossip is the Devil's ware, dear. I don't think you should speak on matters you don't know." She redirected the conversation. "Mason, you still have your fishing gear?"

"Yes ma'am, should be in the garage still."

"Then I think that's a fine idea. The weather will be sunny tomorrow. Why don't the three of you have a lovely day just relaxing on the water, and spend some time catching up."

"Sounds like a plan," agreed Mason. "We'll load up the boat, cruise the inlet, and try an' catch some dinner."

"Let's take it around to Pirate's Bend," Eaver said. "It's not very far from his inlet, and I hear they've been catching lots of channel bass there."

"Okay, we can try that."

"Good," said Sherrie. She was happy that Mason would have a distraction, that her daughter could spend some time with her best friend, and that Danny would be able to spend a day with friends. "It'll be good for all of you."

Tomorrow would be a wonderful day in the cove.

CHAPTER 4

The cat was gone again.

With an irritated sigh, Hannah Dermont pushed open the back patio door, and it responded with its usual gritty creak. The cat was used to nudging the back door open to get outside, and Hannah was sure that was the case now. She peered out into the dark, seeing nothing but a few glowing fireflies in the yard.

"Cappy?" she called. "Caaaaaaappy!"

She was not surprised that the tabby didn't respond. Captain Purrbucket was definitely his own master, unless Hannah was holding him. Then he was a helpless ball of fur with a loud, purring motor.

"Caaaaaaaappy!" she hailed once more. Still no cat came running, and nothing was heard except the noisy chirping of summer locusts in the trees.

Hannah rolled her eyes and huffed in frustration, knowing she could not leave the house until her cat was locked inside. "Dammit, Cappy, I don't have time for this tonight." She stepped out to the back yard to go look for the elusive feline.

She scanned the lawn area for any signs of movement, but he was not there. Next she checked the bushes where Captain Purrbucket sometimes roamed. There was no lurking cat to be found there either.

Pulling her cell phone from her rear pocket, she activated the flashlight app. Then she lit the way before her and proceeded into the wooded area past the lawn.

The foliage was thick at her feet. Making plenty of noise to scare away any potential snakes in the leaves, she walked steadily through the trees.

The light from her phone illuminated the spider webs in her path, which she batted away in disgust. Living in the South, Hannah had dealt with spiders all her life; but walking into a web always freaked her out. It was *yucky*.

And now it was dark, which presented a different trepidation. Hannah grew up walking these woods, and had no problem exploring when she could see everything around her. At night, however, it was a different story. The woods became an obstacle course at night, filled with invisible roots, rocks, critter holes, and sharp branches. Plus there was different animal activity at night, like bats, predatory snakes, and possums. Most were not dangerous, but some certainly could be.

A loud rustling five feet to her left jolted her. She turned her phone light toward the spot.

"Cappy! Kittykittykittykitty!" Nothing moved in the ground foliage. "Goddammit, you stupid cat, I know you're in there. Come here!" Hannah took a step closer.

She heard a low growl.

Startled, she froze in place. That didn't sound like her beloved tabby. She wondered if it was something wild, something mean. Maybe something gone rabid. She needed to be cautious.

Another rustling occurred right behind her. Hannah jumped, then held herself still in case it was a venomous snake positioned by her feet. Her heart was beating robustly now.

A blur exploded out of the brush in front of her. Hannah yelped and convulsed, losing grip of her phone and seeing it fly through the darkness. It landed in a patch of tall bluestem grass.

"Shit!" She hurried to where the phone had fallen, needing to retrieve it while she could still see its light. Reaching down into the wild grass, she wrapped her fingers securely around her phone.

Something struck her back while she was bent over.

Hannah shrieked involuntarily and whirled around. The light from her flashlight app quickly found a familiar face, tan with black and gray striping. It was Captain Purrbucket, pacing the ground in a tight circle.

"Cappy, you little *shit!*" Hannah exclaimed, trying to catch her breath between pounding heartbeats. "Get your ass over here." She stepped to her cat, picked him up, and held him close against her chest.

Just then an ocean breeze pushed its way through the woods to where Hannah was standing. The odor of rotten eggs was on the air, and Hannah wrinkled her nose when it hit her. "What the hell..?"

The tabby growled and burst free from Hannah's arms, springing to the ground. Hannah watched as the cat ran back toward the house.

"Dumb cat," she said to herself. "At least he's headed home." She wasted no time following her pet out of the woods and to the back porch, where he was eagerly waiting to be let inside. She opened the patio door, shooed the cat into the house, and locked the back door behind her.

Now that the cat was safely inside for the night, Hannah could finally finish getting ready to go out. She climbed the stairs to her bedroom and opened her closet to find a blouse. With a wicked smile, she chose a red top with a low neckline. She pulled her T-shirt off, removed her bra, and slipped the blouse on. It lay nicely on her, the neckline exposing plenty of cleavage.

Next she went to her bathroom to check her appearance. After a moment studying herself in the mirror, Hannah decided to put her blonde hair up in side ponytails. Not only would it look cute, but it would also keep her hair from getting too messed up later. Then she applied a little mascara and lipstick, dabbed a bit of perfume on her neck and chest, and she was ready to go.

Hannah grabbed her purse, turned the upstairs lights off, and made her way down the stairs. She gave her mother, who was sitting on the couch, a kiss on the forehead.

"G'night, Ma, I'm going out," said Hannah, heading for the front door.

Her mother produced a look of disappointment. "You're not staying home with me tonight? What are you going to do?"

"Just going out."

"With your friend Eaver?"

"No, Ma."

"Who with, then?"

Hannah simply shook her head. "G'night, Ma. Don't wait up."

CHAPTER 5

Tonight was going to be the night. That was what Walt Echerson Jr. had been telling himself all day. And now that the tent had been set up, the campfire was crackling, and the couple was drinking, he felt more certain of it than ever. This was the night Sarah Primley was finally going to give herself to him.

He had been more than patient. They had been on many dates over the last several weeks, and he had been the perfect gentleman on each occasion. If it were up to him, he would have taken her home on their first date and spent all night ravaging her young, lean body. But she was not that type. She was a trophy that had to be won over, slowly and sweetly. So Walt had taken his time with her. What began with going out to dinner, talking about the things they liked, and getting to know each other had gradually evolved into late-night phone calls, holding hands, and long goodnight kisses.

He had taken some abuse from the crew he ran with. They mocked him and called him a pussy for not yet bedding Sarah. But Walt knew his buddies were savages that would never stand a chance of winning over a beautiful woman like Sarah. So he took their ribbing in stride, focusing on the big picture.

All his time invested was bound to pay off tonight. She had agreed to spend the night camping with him at this secluded point overlooking the surf, the sound of the breaking waves below provided a relaxing, romantic ambiance. The sky above was clear and the stars shone prominently, enhancing the mood even further.

Sarah looked over to Walt, the light from the campfire dancing in her eyes. "Can you get me another drink, please?"

Happy to oblige, Walt reached for her red plastic cup. "Of course. One more Walt Special comin' up." He filled the cup with Red Bull and Jägermeister, swished it around a little, and handed it to Sarah. "Here ya go, sugar."

"Thank you." She took the beverage and brought it to her lips.

Walt watched her lips pucker to the cup, and he imagined how soft and wet they felt. He leaned in to kiss them. Sarah paused for a second, then smiled and pressed her mouth against his. While their lips were locked, he gently laid her down on the wool blanket.

Their kissing became more inspired. But Walt kept the pace steady and controlled, keeping her in her comfort zone. He brought his lips to the nape of her neck. She moaned softly, expressing her pleasure. Whatever perfume she was wearing bore the faint hint of apples, which he liked very much. Walt followed the scent down her body. He began unbuttoning her shirt and kissing her chest.

The smell of her perfume mixed nicely with that of the sweetgrass around them. He could not have set the scene any better if he had to. The stars above, the glow and crackling of the campfire, and the aroma of sweetgrass on the warm breeze created the perfect ambience for this romantic night.

But then the sweet scent was overpowered by a sulfuric odor.

The couple quickly sat up when the smell of rotten eggs hit their noses. "Eww," said Sarah, "what is *that?*"

"I dunno," Walt replied. "I've never smelled anything like that out here before." He scanned the campsite, looking for any sign of something unusual.

A sticky, squishy sound was heard from behind the tent.

Walt stiffened at the sound, and his eyes targeted the small tent. "What the hell?" He slowly stood up, watching diligently. Then he had a thought that angered him. What if the assholes in his crew were there, messing with him like juveniles? This was something he would not stand for; nothing was going to ruin this night.

"Alright, you dickheads," he said. "If you don't get the fuck out of here right now, I'm gonna kick your asses. That goes for you too, Mal!" he added, in case his boss was the culprit.

All was quiet for a minute, then the wet sound returned.

"Okay, you asked for it!" Walt walked fearlessly toward the tent.

Sarah sat up on the blanket, watching Walt with concern. She disliked the guys he hung out with, and if they were here to intrude she would hate them even more. Hopefully it was just some innocent, burrowing critter. She watched Walt make his way to the tent, round the corner behind it, and stop in his tracks.

Then he immediately disappeared from her sight, as if yanked away.

"Walt!" she exclaimed, jumping to her feet. "Walt?"

Nothing was heard but the burning logs popping in the fire.

Sarah tentatively approached the tent. "Dammit Walt, you better not be screwing around. It's not funny." She walked the ten feet cautiously, her body tensing more with each step. She was expecting Walt to spring out from behind the tent and scare her. But he did not.

When she got to the rear of the tent, nobody was there. It was as if Walt had simply been whisked away into the darkness. In the light from the moon she could see the landscape surrounding her. She did not, however, see Walt – or any of his buddies.

And the acrid odor was still in the air.

"Walt! Where are you? Are you okay?" Sarah was confused, frustrated.

A grassy patch rustled in front of her, fifteen feet downhill from the tent.

"Walt?" Sarah moved toward the area. When she got there, she saw what looked like Walt lying on the ground, covered in dark, shiny wetness. And something else.

Something that looked like slimy snakes holding fast to him.

Then a large, conical head thrust out from the grasses and took a big bite out of Walt.

Sarah screamed and her knees wobbled. The thing on the ground took notice, turning a nightmarish face to her. It emerged from the grassy cover and raised itself to meet her wild-eyed stare. Sarah's mind could not comprehend the horror before her, and she was helplessly frozen. Then the inconceivable thing came quickly at her.

Her survival instinct kicked in, and her legs responded. She ran up the hill to the tent, ducked inside, and zipped the opening shut.

She fought to keep utterly still and silent in the dark, despite the blaring fear pulsing through her body. Her ears were perked, listening intently. She heard the terrifying sounds of a slippery nightmare moving alongside the tent. Her heart was racing.

The movement stopped, but Sarah still heard a horrid smacking sound on the other side of the canvas. Then what sounded like snuffling, sniffing.

Suddenly the tent buckled as something began ripping through. Sarah screamed and shrank back against the opposite side of the tent. The light from the campfire showed her glimpses of hooked claws as they tore the tent open, working their way toward her. Realizing she was in a bad position, she scuttled past the intruding creature. While she unzipped the flap with shaking hands, a claw scratched the side of her leg. Screaming wildly, she fled the tent and ran to Walt's truck.

Please, God, she prayed, *let it be unlocked!* If it was locked, she would have to decide whether to go back to Walt's body to search for the keys or to just keep running into the night.

Fortunately, the GMC pickup was unlocked, and she hastily jumped inside. Sarah locked the doors, made sure the windows were rolled up tight, and huddled against the passenger seat. She noticed her leg was itching terribly. Whimpering, she looked through the windshield to see if the thing had followed her.

Something smacked into the passenger door, jolting her. Sarah turned her head to see a hellish face at the glass. The sight stopped her heart for a second. *Jesus, those eyes! Those huge, horrible black eyes!* She tried to scream, but her vocal chords were paralyzed.

The thing struck the window. The glass spiderwebbed and buckled from the blow. Sensing success, the creature hit the window again. This time it shattered inward, covering Sarah with glass fragments.

She raised her arms instinctively to protect her face from the glass. Then she felt something grab – and sharply dig into – her neck and waist. Fighting to breathe with her heart pounding so fiercely, Sarah struggled as best she could.

But all she could do was kick her legs frantically – helplessly – while she was pulled out through the broken window.

CHAPTER 6

Danny Young woke to the sound of birdsong outside his bedroom window. Glancing at the clock on the nightstand, he noticed it was almost eight. Not as late as he had planned to sleep in, but not too early to get up. He decided to mosey down to the kitchen to make some coffee.

His father was sitting at the kitchen table in his flannel bathrobe, slowly nursing a cigarette and sipping coffee. Ricky Young, the prominent owner of one of the town grocery stores, did not look very well. His face was pallid and his eyes puffy. Danny poured himself a cup of coffee and sat beside his father.

"You okay, Dad? You don't look so good."

Ricky grumbled. "Late night doing paperwork at the store. And a little too much to drink afterward." He looked up, following the wispy cigarette smoke, until his bloodshot eyes landed on the dusty chandelier. "You need to clean the house today."

"Yessir," was the only reply Danny could give. Even if he had other plans, it was no use disputing anything his father told him. Especially when he was hung over. Besides, their home could use a little housekeeping.

Ricky brought his eyes back down to his twenty-year-old son. He saw the same blonde curls that Danny's mother had, which was a constant reminder of the failed marriage. "So when are you gonna get a job?"

Danny squirmed in his chair; it was going to be one of those days. "I'm looking, Dad, but there's just not a lot out there right now. Especially that'd work with my school schedule."

"Why don't you quit school so you can find a better job?"

"I'm going to school so I *can* get a better job."

Ricky grumbled again, scratching his graying goatee. "As if that school's gonna help you get a better job. A waste of time and my money, if you ask me." He took a drag from his cigarette.

Despite Danny's urge to argue, he chose to keep the peace. The only one who was ever right in Ricky's house was Ricky. This was a lesson Danny had learned all his life. He simply said, "Don't worry, Dad, I'll do you proud. You'll see."

Not that anything Danny did ever made Ricky proud. Whatever minor triumphs, accolades, or accomplishments Danny had, they were never met with any acknowledgement from his father. In Ricky's eyes, nobody would ever measure up to his own level.

Ricky had done well with his life. Nobody could deny his work ethic; he always worked hard and made money. When he was thirty he was able to get a bank loan to buy one of the town grocery stores. It was the smaller of the two stores, but was a money maker nonetheless. After many diligent years, he paid back the loan and finally started stashing profits into his retirement fund. Ricky was now financially comfortable and in control of his own future.

He had even taken a stab at public office, running for sheriff one year. Unfortunately he lost the election to Jimmy Steele, who was still the sheriff to this day. Sheriff Steele was the most qualified candidate, by far, but Ricky was still bitter about losing. "Sumbitch only won because'a his name," Ricky would always say. "Sheriff Steele... it's a winner."

Seeing his father's coffee cup almost empty, Danny stood from the table and went to the coffee maker. He grabbed the steaming pot and brought it back to the table. "Need a topper, Dad?"

Ricky grunted and nodded. He finished his cigarette and squashed it in the ashtray, then lit another while Danny poured the coffee.

They quietly read the Sunday paper for a while. Then the telephone rang. Ricky winced a little from the sound, and Danny promptly sprang from the table to answer it. "Hello?"

"Hey, Danny, whatcha doin'?" said the familiar voice of Eaver.

"Hey, Eaver. Not much, just havin' some coffee. What're you up to?"

"Seein' if you want to hang out today. Mason's back, you know, and I'm taking him fishing. We'd like you to come with."

"Yeah, that'd be cool. Perfect day for it, too," he added, glancing out the window at the sunny morning. "I'm sure he could use a fun day out; I heard about his momma."

"So when can we come over? Maybe we can go out on the boat?"

"Hang on, I'll check. Hey Dad," he called, his hand covering the receiver. "It's Eaver Robinson. You remember Mason Parker, the one whose mom just died? Well, Eaver's taking him fishing today, and they want me to go along. Is that cool with you?"

Despite wanting to make his son stay home and clean, the idea of having a quiet house to himself appealed to Ricky. He could spend the day lying on the couch and recovering from his hangover. "Yeah, go on ahead. You can clean the house later, I suppose."

"Sure, Eaver, come on over. I can be ready in half an hour. Y'all have your poles?"

"Yes we do. Do we need to bring anything else?"

"Naw, I'll load up the cooler with stuff. See ya when you get here." Danny hung up. "Thanks, Dad. I haven't seen Mason since high school. It'll be nice to catch up."

"He just graduated college, didn't he? Ask him to help you find a job."

Danny rolled his eyes and clenched his teeth, saying nothing. Instead of replying, he thought about how nice it would be to get out of the house for the day, away from his reproachful father. Then he had a great idea.

He had been infatuated with Hannah Dermont for years, since trying to date her in high school. But she had denied his advances every time, causing him to want her even more. Lately he had abandoned his pursuit of her, but he still thought about her constantly. Going fishing with Mason and Eaver today was a perfect opportunity to call her and ask her to join them. Perhaps she would be more comfortable spending time with him in the company of other friends.

Danny dialed Hannah's number and waited patiently for her to pick up. After six rings she finally answered. "Hullo?"

"Hannah? Hey, it's me, Danny."

Her voice was groggy. "What time is it?"

"I dunno, eight-thirty or so. I'm going fishing today with Eaver and Mason Parker, and we thought you might like to come along."

"Jesus, Danny, I dunno… I feel like shit. I ain't going anywhere today."

Danny noted the same tone that his wrecked father had. "What, did *everyone* get wasted last night?"

"Huh?"

"Never mind, just get better, I guess. I'll talk with you later."

"M'kay." Hannah hung up.

Danny shrugged. His attempts to see her were thwarted once again, but at least he would still have a good time on the boat today. He went upstairs for a quick shower.

Eaver and Mason arrived a short time later, fishing gear in hand. Danny greeted them from the front porch, where he was packing food and drink into a fiberglass cooler. Danny stood and shook Mason's hand when he approached.

"How're you doin', Mason?"

"Okay, Danny. How've you been?"

"Aw, you know. Just pluggin' forward. I should graduate community college next year, find a decent job, and get the hell outta here." Danny turned to glance at the shallow inlet at the edge of the back yard. "Come on now, let's do some fishing!"

"Hell yeah," Eaver concurred. "I say we hit Pirate's Bend for some channel bass."

Mason carried the poles and tackle box while Danny grabbed a cooler and led his friends down to the water's edge. They got to the rowboat, which was kept bottom-up to keep the inside dry, and kicked the hull to scare away any snakes that might be sleeping in the shade underneath. Then Eaver helped Danny roll the boat over and drag it to the water.

"We got everything we need?" Mason asked, setting the fishing gear in the boat.

"Yep, in the cooler. We got sodas, waters, jerky, and peanuts from Bennie's. And a glass for my peanuts and Coke."

Eaver rolled her eyes. "You and your peanuts and Coke."

Mason, who also enjoyed the Southern combination, chortled. "No worse than your ketchup fetish. Heck, you'd probably do peanuts and ketchup!"

She laughed until she snorted. "Hush it! You're all sorts of wrong." She looked at Danny. "You did bring a bottle of ketchup, didn't you?"

Danny just shook his head. "That's enough out of you both. Let's get this expedition moving."

They loaded the boat and stepped inside. Danny unstrapped the pair of plastic oars that were secured to the side of the boat. He took one for himself and handed the other one to Mason. Then they pushed the craft away from shore and began paddling out.

As they glided across the inlet, Mason watched the shimmering tips of sunlight reflecting on the water. He smiled, feeling peaceful. This was exactly what he needed.

"So whatcha gonna do now that you're home from college?" asked Danny while they rowed.

"I'm not sure. I was going to try to find a job in the city after the summer, which I guess I still could. But with Momma dying, I have to focus on other stuff here."

"Yeah, I suppose so. I was really sorry to hear about her passing."

Mason nodded. "Yep." He took a moment to keep from tearing up. "Yeah, it's really hard right now."

Eaver rested a hand on his knee. "I'm sorry, sugar. It'll get better."

"I know, I know. Just gotta keep looking forward. Shoot, I have to go see the lawyer tomorrow and get everything with her will squared away. Thank God the house was paid for, that'll be a big help not having to worry about that. But I'll have to find a job here if I stay in the house."

"Or sell it," Danny pointed out, "and use the money to buy something else in whatever area you end up working."

Mason shrugged. "We'll see. I kinda like it here. There's something to be said for living in a small, quiet town. Simple living."

"Amen," said Eaver. "You should stay here. You've still got your friends."

"That I do," Mason acknowledged. "And I wouldn't have it any other way." He continued pulling the oar, turning his head to watch the swirling current left by each stroke.

Eaver redirected the focus on Danny. "So, is your dad still

being a dick?"

Danny smirked, a little ashamed. "Yes'm, unfortunately. Still an unbearable control freak."

Eaver remembered Ricky's temperament all too well. "Last time I saw ol' 'King Richard' I had to watch while he made you stand in the corner, nose pressed to the wall, for talking back to him. I was so embarrassed for you that all I could do was sit on the couch and wait quietly until he let you go with me."

"Jesus," said Mason. "Does he think you're still six years old?"

"He's always been kind of a dick to me. I'm not sure why, but I suspect that I was an accident. Maybe deep down he's always resented me for making him settle down with Mom to raise a baby. And it didn't help matters when she left him a few years back." Danny then chuckled. "I'm thinking she had the right idea."

"Hang in there, Danny," Mason reassured. "Like you said, next year you'll graduate and get the hell outta there."

The group reached the coast, steered south, and paddled alongshore. Before long, they had reached the mouth of Pirate's Bend. They brought the boat to the center of the quiet cove and stopped there.

While rigging his fishing pole, Danny noticed an area of the shoreline squared off by yellow police tape. "What happened over there, I wonder?"

Mason followed Danny's eyes to the spot on shore, then immediately remembered what he had overheard at the funeral. "Oh yeah, the sheriff was talking about some bloody something found here. They think it might be from ol' Earl."

"No shit," Danny muttered.

Eaver cringed. "You mean like something in the water got him?"

"That's what I'd imagine," said Mason. "Anything in here that would attack and kill a man?" he asked Danny.

"*Duh-dum, duh-dum,*" he sang ominously, and the others immediately recognized the theme from Jaws.

"Very funny," said Eaver. "You do know that sharks can get in here."

"Of course," Danny replied nonchalantly. "Probably coming up for the boat as we speak."

Mason laughed, but the statement had triggered fear in him.

"But seriously," added Danny, "no. I don't know what could'a happened to ol' Earl. He was a capable man of the water, so I'm at a loss." He glanced again at the police tape on the shoreline.

A sound in the water was heard, perhaps twenty yards from the rowboat. It was not so much a splash, but more like the sound of something slipping under the water.

The group looked in that direction, but saw nothing but ripples on the surface. They studied the water in quiet nervousness.

Eaver looked down into the murky green next to the boat. All she could see were rays of sunlight fading into the cloudy depths and disappearing a few feet down. Below that nothing was visible. The fact that anything could be swimming down there made Eaver shudder.

"What do you say we paddle back to Danny's inlet?" she suggested. "There's good fishing there too."

A slight breeze blew across the water and up Mason's neck, giving him goosebumps. He nodded. "Sounds good to me. Let's get out of here."

CHAPTER 7

The midday sun welcomed Mason when he finally emerged from the courthouse. He had been busy since nine this morning, starting with meeting his mother's lawyer, going through procedural paperwork, and ending with him in the courthouse filing for letters of testamentary. After three hours of being smothered in details over the will, death certificates, and everything he would need to do over the next couple of weeks, the sun on his face felt like a reward.

Mason still had much to do. He would need to find his mother's insurance policy, credit card statements, checking, savings, and investment accounts, inform those companies of her passing, and transfer the accounts with the water and utility companies to his name. But he felt like he had done enough for one day. Now he needed to do something enjoyable.

He thought about going to Sherrie's Shack. He would have a nice lunch there, in a familiar, friendly atmosphere. Then perhaps he and Eaver could run off and do something together. Satisfied with his plan, he headed to the restaurant.

Sherrie's Shack stood near the beach, a few hundred feet north of the dock. The name did indeed suit the modest sized restaurant, which looked like a shack. Its walls were comprised of weathered cedar shingles and it was covered in corrugated metal roofing. But the large windows, festive awnings, and the brightly-painted sign above the door cemented its appearance as that of a local restaurant.

The welcome smells of Southern cooking struck Mason instantly when he entered. His nose picked up the smoky barbeque, the sautéed shrimp, the chowder, and the chicken in the fryer. He was now hungrier than ever.

"Hey, sweetie!" said Sherrie from behind the counter, unconsciously brushing the front of her patterned apron. "How are you today?"

Mason smiled, hanging his sunglasses on the neckline of his T-shirt. "Very well, Ms. Sherrie. Smells damn good in here."

"Well, duh!" Sherrie placed her hand on her hips. "Would you expect anything less?"

"No, ma'am, I wouldn't." Mason scanned the floor for Eaver, spotting her wiping down one of the tables. She glanced at him, smiling sweetly. "I was thinking about stealing Eaver away from you for a bit, but after lunch of course."

"Don't see why not. It's a beautiful day out." She was pleased that young Mason wanted to take her daughter out for a while. "So what can I get ya for lunch?"

"Well, I was thinking about the fried chicken plate. And does Cinch have any of his awesome gumbo made?"

"Yes sir," she confirmed. Then she turned her head back toward the kitchen. "Hey Cinch, this fella here says he wants some of your gumbo."

A seventy-year-old black man popped his head around the wall. He had a head full of short, gray curls, and sideburns to match. When he recognized Mason, his eyes lit up and a broad smile stretched across his leathery face. "Dat be young Mr. Mason! I was wondering when you would be in to see us!" He walked out to the counter. "It's good to see you, boy!"

Mason's heart warmed when he heard the old Creole's familiar voice. Mason had spent many years in the company of ol' Cinch, who had cooked for Sherrie in the restaurant since Mason was a child. Cinch was the closest thing he had to a grandfather. "Good to see you too, Cinch. It's been a while." Mason extended his hand, and Cinch reached out with both of his thin arms to grasp it.

"I got a good gumbo today, boy. Lemme tell you. You gonna love it."

"I can't wait, ol' buddy." He watched the old man scurry back to the kitchen to dish his cooking.

"And a chicken plate," said Sherrie. Then she turned to Mason, gave a refusing gesture when he reached for his wallet, and told him to be seated.

Minutes later Sherrie brought his meal to him, with Eaver right behind carrying the drink and silverware. Sherrie set the plate down before him, and then the steaming bowl next to that. The freshly fried chicken looked and smelled amazing. "How's that look for ya?"

"Well, it's no Bojangles'," Mason teased, "but it'll do."

Sherrie gasped. "You hush it! I should pinch you."

Mason and Eaver giggled at her reaction. "You know I'm just playin', Sherrie. Looks delicious, as always."

Sherrie mussed his red hair a bit. "Enjoy your lunch, Trouble."

He dug into his food, realizing after his first bite just how famished he was. The comfort food revitalized his body and soul. He was soon full and content.

When he was finished, Eaver cleared the table and carted the dishes to the kitchen. Then she returned to his table and seated herself opposite him. "So what's the plan, Stan?"

"I dunno, Eave. Just thought we'd hang out and do whatever today. What would you like to do?"

Eaver smacked her palms lightly on the table top. "Let's go get some ice cream! I'm craving something cold and sweet."

"Okay," Mason said with a nod. "That sounds damn good right now. Is Rosie's still here?"

"You know it. Been here as long as anyone can remember, and probably will be forever."

Mason pushed his chair back and stood. "Then let's go. My treat."

Eaver popped up and took Mason's hand, heading for the door. "We're going out, Momma," she called to Sherrie. "I don't know when I'll be back." Sherrie waved them off with a smile, and the couple exited the restaurant.

They walked south for a block, along a row of magnolia trees. The trees were full with waxy, dark green leaves and giant white flowers. The scent from the blooms was perfume in the thick summer air. Mason felt happy.

The friends turned onto Main Street and followed the sidewalk inland several blocks until they found themselves in front of the ice cream parlor, Rosie's Creamery. They met with a soothing blast of air conditioning when they stepped inside. Eaver eagerly led Mason to the display case to decide on a flavor.

Old Rosie was at the counter as always, still loving her chosen profession. She greeted the couple with a pleasant smile and asked what she could serve up for them. Mason bought two sugar cones, with cookies and cream for him and butter pecan for Eaver, and then the two sat down to enjoy their gourmet ice creams. When they were finished, they thanked Rosie, who waved and wished them a blessed day.

Once outside, they paused on the sidewalk while Mason put on his sunglasses.

"What should we do now?" Eaver asked.

"I'm game for whatever, what sounds good to you?"

She tilted her head. "We could get some cold beers, head down to the creek, and do some fishing under the trees."

"Are you even old enough to buy beer yet?"

The young lady batted her eyelashes. "Will be next year."

"Hey, Eaver-Beaver!" a brusque voice hailed.

Mason turned his head to see who had called out, and his heart skipped a beat.

It was the dreaded Malcolm Gibbs, known to all as Big Mal. Malcolm was Mason's age – but bigger and tougher – and had been the class bully throughout their entire school career in Sweetboro.

Mal was on the other side of the street with two of his usual friends, Mitch Haverson and Jesse Reed. Having caught the attention of Eaver and Mason, they crossed the street to engage them. Mason could feel his adrenaline building as they approached. Mal's appearance was intimidating; he stood an inch or two taller than Mason, had long, slicked-back black hair, and a square jaw. He looked every bit as big and mean as Mason remembered.

"Hey, Mal," Eaver acknowledged.

"How you doin', girl?" Mal looked at Mason. "Haven't seen you in a long time, Red."

"Hey, Mal. Been away at college."

"So you're a fancy college boy, huh?" He leaned in closer to the smaller young man.

"I suppose," Mason replied, avoiding direct eye contact. "I just moved back after graduation. What's new with you?"

Mal relaxed his stance. "Livin' large and in charge. Makin' money, money, money!" He raised his hand for a high-five from one of his associates, which he promptly received. Then his face grew a little sterner. "Have either of you seen Walt Echerson?"

Mason and Eaver shook their heads. "No, Mal," said Eaver, "not recently."

"Well, I need him for work and he ain't nowhere to be found. Not answerin' his phone, neither. Let him know I'm lookin' for him if'n you see him, Eaver-Beaver."

Eaver winced. "Aww, that name never gets old, Mal," she smiled sarcastically. "Maybe Walt finally decided to grow up and stop hanging around Neanderthals."

Mal puffed up angrily. "What the fuck's *that* supposed to mean?"

Confrontation with Big Mal was the last thing Mason wanted; he quickly diffused the situation. "C'mon, Eaver, let's go look for him. We'll tell him to call you if we see him, Mal. Okay?"

Mal directed his stare at Mason. "Yeah," he said after a silent moment. Then, with a jab of his finger to Mason's chest, he added, "You do that, Red." Then Big Mal took his buddies back across the street to resume their day.

Mason waited until they were out of earshot before he commented. "What a dick! God, I *hate* Mal! Still an asshole, I see."

"Oh yes," said Eaver. "He hasn't changed a bit. Except maybe becoming more of a thug."

"I see he still hangs with the same crew of troublemakers from high school."

"His same ol' posse. But now, instead of stealing lunch money, they grow pot somewhere on the hill and sell it."

Mason was shocked. "No shit?" He was surprised to hear of anyone growing illegal marijuana, even a degenerate such as Big Mal. "That's crazy. And the sheriff doesn't know?"

"Naw, Mal is at least smart enough not to shit where he eats. He and his little gang sell to nearby towns. Nobody around here is really affected by it."

"Huh." Mason processed his thoughts for a moment, evaluating what Malcolm Gibbs had amounted to. The bully who had menaced him for years was still just that, and now a drug dealer as well. All the more reason to stay away from Big Mal.

Mason snapped back to the moment at hand. "C'mon, Eave. Let's go back to my car, go get that beer, and do that fishing."

CHAPTER 8

Danny felt drained. The last hour had been a combination of scrubbing, washing, and having to listen to NASCAR from the TV in the next room. The constant droning of race cars was not a pleasant companion to his toil. But per his father's direction, Danny was to clean the house today. So he tackled the task, NASCAR noise and all.

He had the kitchen floor, cabinets, and counters looking spick and span, and was now working on the dusty chandelier above the kitchen table. Standing on one of the chairs, he took a washcloth to the dangling crystals and wiped them shiny. When he was finished, he stepped down and pushed the chair back in.

"Okay, Dad," he called to the living room, "kitchen and dining room are done."

After a few seconds, the TV volume was turned down. "Did you get the chandelier?"

"Yep, just now. Do you wanna come look?"

Ricky pulled himself up from the couch cushion. "Awright, let's see how you did." He appeared from around the corner, immediately scanning the kitchen, ceiling, and dining table. Everything looked clean, but he noticed a smudge on the table. "You missed a spot," he said, directing with his eyes.

Danny moved to catch the right angle, then saw what his father saw. "So I did. No worries, I'll get it." He reached for the furniture polish and dust rag. "Then would it be cool if I go out with my friends?"

Ricky rolled his eyes. "You did that yesterday. Remember, instead of cleaning the house like I told you to?"

"Well, yeah, but you told me I could. And I cleaned it today."

"Some, but you're not even close to being done. There's still the living room, the bathrooms, and the laundry."

Danny felt deflated. "All that?"

"I told you, you're cleaning the house today." Ricky looked at his burdensome son with contempt, then buried his face in his hands. "Why are you so goddamn lazy? Is this how hard you look for jobs too?"

Danny could feel anger rising in him, but he knew better than to show it. He kept his voice peaceful. "Dad, if me working is so important to you, then why don't you just give me a job at the store?"

Ricky shook his head. This topic had come up on several occasions before, and he had denied it each time. The last thing he wanted was to hire his son to work at his grocery store. For several reasons.

"For the last time, that's not gonna happen. You need to find your own way, not rely on me all your life. Plus, I can't show favoritism among my employees."

"You wouldn't have to, I'd have the same expectations –"

Ricky waved his hand violently in the air, indicating he wanted nothing to do with this debate. "No. That's the end of it."

Danny sighed. "Okay, whatever."

The reaction triggered ire in Ricky. He took a step closer to his son. "What's that? You have an attitude today?"

The confrontational behavior made Danny's pulse quicken. "No sir, I just don't understand. It seems like I can't make you happy, no matter what. I go to school so I can get a good job someday, I do chores around the house, and I even offer to work for you."

"Just clean the house today, and shut up about it."

"I will. But afterward I need to spend some time with Eaver and Mason before –"

"No, what you *need* to do is what you're told. Am I clear?"

The submissive son sprayed the table and began wiping it clean.

Ricky brought his face right to Danny's ear. "I said, am I *clear?*"

Danny nodded. "Yessir."

"And another thing –"

"Aren't you going to work today?"

"Watch that smart mouth, boy," Ricky warned, his voice rising with the same intimidating tone he had used for many years. "You're not too big for me to lay a whooping on."

Danny wondered – for the shortest of moments – if he was big enough to stand up to his old man. He could surely take a beating, as he had done on occasion over the years. But then he decided his father was still too tough, too belligerent, too strong for even a twenty-year-old to take on. Besides, Danny needed a place to call home until he was out of school and could provide for himself. So he cowered, as he always had. "Yessir," he said obediently.

"I don't know why I put up with you, Danny. I really don't. You don't work, don't pay bills, eat my food, live under my roof, and you bitch about having to do a little work around here instead of fucking around with your friends."

Danny did not respond; instead, he continued wiping down the table. He was upset about the way his father was treating him, and had always treated him, but he knew there was no point trying to communicate his feelings. Danny's feelings didn't matter to Ricky, all that mattered was Ricky's rule. So Danny kept his feelings bottled up, as usual, and kept working.

Ricky stood quietly, then looked down at his watch. "As a matter of fact," he noted, "I do need to go to the store and check in on everyone working today." He retreated to the living room to turn the TV off and grab his cell phone and keys. "I'll be back in a few hours," Ricky stated. "And when I get back, you better have this whole goddamn house clean. Is that understood? Am I *clear?*"

"Yessir."

Ricky left the house, started his truck, and drove away. When the sound of the motor was gone, Danny reared his head back and yelled at the ceiling. *"AAAARRGH! You're CLEAR, 'King Richard', you're CLEAR! You're such a fucking asshole!"* The outburst released some of the frustration that was boiling inside him.

Danny stewed for ten minutes. Then, with a sigh, he resumed his cleaning duties while secretly wishing his resentful father was dead.

CHAPTER 9

Sheriff Jimmy Steele sat behind his desk, stroking his bushy mustache in deep thought. Earl Goates was still missing, as were any new clues to what had happened to him. All they had to go on was the damaged dinghy found on the rocks, blood spatter on the inside and outside boards, and the long tooth embedded in the boat's underside.

Marty Bennett, the resident diver and authority on marine life, had searched the turbid waters of the cove for hours on Saturday. But the diver had found no body, nor any evidence of one. The old fisherman had simply vanished from the face of the earth.

The fact that Earl had no family saddened the sheriff. If Earl turned up dead, nobody would be there to mourn him and give him a funeral. But at least the sheriff would not have to endure the discomfort of informing family members that Earl had died.

His eyes drifted to the picture frame perched on his desk. The brass lattice held a warm photo of the thirty-seven-year-old sheriff, his wife Betty, and his two boys Jack and Mark. If anything ever happened to him, his family would be devastated. But at least he would be remembered. Poor Earl would eventually be forgotten completely.

Deputy Carl Riggins walked in with two cups of coffee and noticed the furrowed brow of his boss. "Thinking about Earl?" he ventured.

The sheriff nodded in the affirmative. "We should've found a body by now. Currents wouldn't carry it out of the cove, not the way they flow into there. Unless he's just gone missing – but the blood and scratched-up boat suggest otherwise."

"Like I said, looked like an animal attack."

"Yeah, it's looking that way. I want to know what that tooth came from."

Carl set the coffees down and seated himself on the opposite side of the desk. "Have you heard back from Marty yet?"

"No, not yet. I guess he's taking his time identifying it."

"We may need him to dive again and keep searching," the deputy suggested.

"Maybe, Spud. Maybe."

The phone on the desk rang, and Sheriff Steele glanced down at the caller ID. The incoming call was from Marty Bennett, the diver.

"Speak of the devil." The sheriff picked up using speakerphone. "Steele here."

"Hi, Sheriff, it's Marty."

"Howdy, Marty. What's up?"

"You know that object you found in the boat hull?"

"Yep. Sand tiger tooth?"

"Um, no. That's what's got me so mystified. It's not a tooth."

The sheriff was stunned. He took a moment to process the statement before responding. "What? What the hell else could it be?"

"I originally thought it was from a sand tiger too, seeing as they like shallow waters. But their teeth are more blade-like whereas this is more cylindrical. And the shark teeth have a bilobed root, but this doesn't. And it doesn't have a nutrient groove in the center either. So I wondered if it could be a claw."

"A *claw?* No way."

"I took it over to the lab to have it analyzed. Based on the amount of hard keratin, and the things I already mentioned, they confirmed my suspicion that it's actually a claw."

"So could it've been a gator?" Carl asked, grinning proudly since he had suggested alligators as possible culprits when they investigated the scene.

"No, although they did find marine reptile DNA. But it's nothing like an alligator claw. And the DNA was more consistent with that of benthic life."

The sheriff rolled his eyes. Marty always did like showing off his knowledge of marine biology. "What's that mean in layman's terms, Marty?"

"Means whatever it came from probably lives on the ocean floor. But it has claws – which means digits, which means limbs – which implies it could operate on land as well."

Sheriff Steele buried his face in his hands. "Are you trying to tell me nobody knows what this tooth – claw – came from?"

"Afraid so. We've compared it to everything that lives in necrotic zone and nothing matches. This thing has me baffled."

"Alrighty then, I guess we're back to square one on what happened to old Earl."

"Maybe," said Marty. "I'm gonna dive Pirate's Bend again. I have to see if I can find anything that leads me to what this claw came from."

The sheriff squirmed at the thought of somebody diving in waters shared with an unknown danger, but he knew it had to be done. "I suppose we'll need you to. Just be careful in there. You bringin' additional divers with you? Or spearguns or something?"

"Naw, I don't think that's necessary. Whatever has claws like this is probably a nocturnal predator. I should be just fine during the day. Just like I was last time."

The sheriff nodded to the blind speakerphone. "Alrighty then, when're you planning on diving?"

"This afternoon. I just need to gather my gear and fill my tanks, but I'll be back in that water as soon as I possibly can."

CHAPTER 10

It was half past three when Marty arrived at Pirate's Bend. He still had plenty of good daylight left to thoroughly search the water in the cove. He parked his van on the side of the road, then got in the back to get ready for his dive.

He took his shirt and shorts off and slipped into his neoprene wetsuit. Then he donned his weight belt and strapped his dive knife around his leg. Opening the side door, he emerged from the van with his mask, tank, and fins in hand.

With care, he walked barefoot down the rocky embankment to the water's edge. There he sat, pulled the fins over his feet, and strapped the air tank to his back. Then he cleaned his mask with spit and seawater and positioned it tightly onto his face. Finally, he stepped into the water and kicked away from the shore. After a quick test of his mouthpiece and regulator, Marty dove beneath the surface.

The water was murky, brown with turbidity. Marty's eyes focused on the particles of sediment and zooplankton, watching the current pull them back and forth. He studied the endless motion for a minute, then returned his thoughts to the task at hand. He began to swim over the floor of the cove, searching for further clues as to what kind of animal had attacked the fisherman and his dinghy.

Marty spent thirty-five minutes underwater, scouring the area for signs of a predator. But in that time he found nothing useful in the rock and sand. Disgruntled, he was about to return to the surface when something caught his eye.

His search had brought him to a tight notch in the corner of the cove. A small area – darker than the rest of the stony seascape – stood out in the haze, about fifteen feet below. He swam nearer to it. Upon a closer look, Marty discovered the dark patch was actually the entrance to an underwater cave.

Aha! he thought. Perhaps the answers that eluded him would be found inside the cave. But that was something he could not explore at the moment. He would need his flashlight, which was in the van, and he was due for a new air tank. Marty surfaced, took note of where he was, and swam back to where his van was parked.

After retrieving his flashlight and replacing his harness with a full air tank, Marty returned to the water. He eagerly headed back to the notch of the cove where he had seen the dark opening of the cave. Then he bit onto his mouthpiece and kicked his way down below the waves.

The opening was just big enough for Marty and his gear to slip through. It was pitch black inside, so he could not tell if it was any more spacious farther in. There was only one way to find out. Activating the flashlight and holding it in front of him, he gave a kick of his flippers and pulled himself inside with his free hand.

Cave diving was something Marty had done many times before, so he was well aware of the potential dangers. He had a full air tank, his diving knife, knew to avoid areas he or his gear could get trapped in, and would keep himself wary of any currents within. As long as he took it slow and cautious, he would be fine.

The flashlight illuminated the tunnel before him. The walls, consisting of limestone and other sedimentary rock, were bumpy but smooth, having been eroded by thousands of years of flowing water. Some sand and silt danced on the bottom, giving Marty an indication of the strength and direction of the current. Twenty feet in, the cave grew larger, giving Marty room to move around more freely.

He was now in a chamber that was twelve feet in diameter. The spaciousness around him made him feel more relaxed, as did the softening of the current. There was still no sign of Earl Goates's body, nor evidence of any animal that might have attacked the old fisherman.

Marty continued kicking, pushing himself forward. He went another thirty feet, then stopped. He could see a weak light ahead. Curious, he swam toward it.

He was soon in the pocket of a large cavern. Seeing the light dance above him, he followed it until he broke the surface and found air again. Marty removed his mask and looked around to study his surroundings.

The cavern was breathtaking. Its high walls stretched upward to converge on a small hole in the rock, where the daylight was coming in. The ceiling was covered with calcium stalactites protruding down, twenty feet in some cases. To complement them, towering stalagmites reached up from the rocky floor. The enormous chamber was quiet, dark, and warm... aside from the lingering stink of sulfur, it brought a sense of tranquility and peace.

Marty studied the hole at the top. It looked like a natural blowhole, caused by millennia of erosion. Gauging his whereabouts, he figured he must be underneath Pirate's Point, the scenic spot overlooking Pirate's Bend. And the hole letting light inside the cavern had to be the same fenced-off hole in the rock on top of Pirate's Point. All this time he had no idea of the beauty that had been hidden from the outside world.

Marty kicked to the edge of the rock and pulled himself out of the water. Leaving his flippers on, he cautiously began walking to explore the grotto. He was careful to watch where he was going, noting the calcium stumps and flowstone on the floor.

About ten feet from the water, he found a flat area of floor that was covered in seaweed and kelp. *Odd*, he thought. *How would seaweed gather in one concentrated spot?* Even in high tide, anything that had washed in would be left scattered as the water receded. This seemed more deliberate than natural. It resembled a den.

Marty moved past the seaweed and resumed his exploration. He moved along another ten feet to the corner of the cavern. Where the floor eventually met the rocky wall, Marty spotted something unusual.

There was a hollow in the rock, about six feet across, that was full of ocean water. But what truly puzzled Marty was what he saw inside the hollow. There were dozens of oblong objects, a mere foot beneath the surface, resting in the crater. With the aid of his flashlight he was able to see more detail. They were a greenish-yellow color, the texture looked leathery, and they were the size of footballs.

They looked like *eggs*.

The sulfur smell grew a little stronger. Marty took notice, prompting his thoughts to shift to wondering if there was a natural hot spring down here. It would be unprecedented for the area, which piqued his urge to search for the odor's suspected source. The orbs in the pool could wait for now.

Marty scanned the floor of the cavern with his flashlight, but could not find a single hot spring. Nor did he see evidence of the yellow sulfur that should be there to give off that distinct smell. Perplexed, he circled back to revisit the mysterious leathery orbs.

Stepping alongside the water's edge to avoid as many stalagmites as possible, he made his way toward the puzzling pool. Then, behind him, the gentle sounds of splashing and lapping were heard in the quiet of the cavern.

Was that something slipping into the water?

…Or out?

His eyes darting nervously, Marty scanned the cavern for any movement. He saw none. But he could hear something, now coming from more than one location. Wet, sticky sounds from something brushing the rocks around him. And the sounds were converging on him. He started thinking the sheriff may have been right – maybe Marty should've brought a speargun after all.

In the light from the hole above, movement caught Marty's eye. He drew in on it to see a silhouette. But he could not quite make out what it was. *That's fucked up*, he thought, *it almost looks like a walking octopus.*

Staying at the edge of the water, he aimed his flashlight to illuminate the creature. There was nothing there now. Marty frowned, bewildered. Could the thing have been a marine creature? A reptile? Or could it be some mammal like a wildcat or big possum? Whatever it was, it was probably not friendly. And he could still hear movement on the rock around him.

He had to get out of there.

Pinning the flashlight in his armpit to free his shaky hands, Marty hastily donned his facemask and mouthpiece. Then he dove back into the water to flee the cavern.

His heart racing, he swam as quickly as he could. He took quick looks behind him every few seconds, making sure nothing was following. To his relief, the flashlight beam revealed nothing in the briny giving chase.

Marty made his way back to the cove and surfaced. Then he hurried out of the water to get to the van and report his findings to the sheriff.

CHAPTER 11

Sheriff Steele was about to sneak home for dinner when he got the call. Being the only person in the station, as Carl Riggins was out patrolling and old Lewis Simkins wouldn't be shuffling in for another couple of hours to start the next shift, he answered the ringing telephone.

"Sheriff Steele here," he announced into the mouthpiece.

"Hey Sheriff," said a man on the other end, "we found us an abandoned truck up here on the hills near Pirate's Point."

"Okay, any idea whose it is?"

"I'm pretty sure it's Walt Echerson Jr.'s GMC."

"Anybody see young Walt?"

"No, Sheriff. And that's why I called. There's a tore-up tent here, camping gear everywhere, but nobody around. And the truck has a window busted out with what looks like blood on it."

Steele's ears perked. What he assumed was a typical truck-ran-out-of-gas situation had suddenly become a potential crime scene. "Who is this?" he asked.

"Donnie Broden," the man informed. "We was just hikin' the ridge and we saw this mess up here. Didn't look good, so I figured I'd better call you."

"Thank you, Donnie, I appreciate that. Do me a favor, will ya? Don't touch anything, try to leave everything exactly how you found it. I'm on my way right now. Can you hang out there for a few and wait for me?"

"Sure, Sheriff."

"Great. Now where exactly are you?"

"Just a few hundred yards past Pirate's Point, past the rocks, right where you can overlook the beach down that long hill to the estuary."

"Got it. I'll find you in about ten minutes, Donnie. And thanks again for the call."

He hung up, then called Carl on the radio to bring him back to the station. While the deputy was on his way in, the sheriff phoned his wife to inform her that he would be unable to join the family for dinner tonight. She sighed, disappointed, but she understood being married to a policeman. Next the sheriff called Deputy Simkins to have him come in a couple hours early to man the station.

By the time Carl pulled in, Sheriff Steele was waiting by the door. He met his deputy at the driver side window.

"We got a call, Spud," the sheriff announced. "Take us up to Pirate's Point."

"You got it," said Carl. The sheriff stepped around to the passenger side and got into the cruiser. Then Deputy Riggins drove them away.

"Did you get some dinner yet?" asked the deputy.

"No. I was about to when Donnie Broden called."

"Well, I'm hungry. Wanna run to Sherrie's with me after this?"

"Depends on how long this'll take, Spud."

"What are we checking out?"

The sheriff told him about the discovery of Walt's damaged truck and the described condition of the campsite around it. By the time Carl was brought up to speed, they were at Pirate's Bend and almost to the hill leading to Pirate's Point. Sheriff Steele glanced at the cove as they passed by, and the waves breathing together in the waning daylight made the cove appear to be a single, living entity. For a moment the sight made him think about the lives Pirate's Bend had taken over the years. Like it had fed on them.

Deputy Riggins steered up the short road that ended at the top of Pirate's Point. From there the two policemen exited the car and began walking the trail to the secluded side of the hills where the campsite was found. After five minutes of silent trekking, they saw the ridge where the truck was. Several men were standing there, waiting.

Donnie Broden, a Sweetboro native, wore a troubled face. "Howdy, Sheriff. Glad you're here, this don't look good." He gestured to the truck. "Looks like some foul play took place here."

Sheriff Steele approached the light-blue GMC, noticing the broken window and the pieces of glass on the ground below. The passenger side window was gone, save the remaining shards that protruded from the frame. The sheriff could see blood on the edges of the jagged glass. Looking closer, he also saw blood spatter on the dashboard and steering wheel.

"We got blood, Spud."

The deputy opened the driver side door and examined the interior. "Sure do. Somebody got cut or shot in here, and then dragged out through that window, leaving the broken glass bloody."

The sheriff took a step back, looking at the ground. Seeing nothing but grass and dirt, he knelt down for a better look. "I don't see a blood trail leading away anywhere," he said, his voice perplexed.

"We kinda looked around the whole area," said Donnie. "You know, to see if there was a body."

"And nothing?"

"Nothing. Then we decided to quit pokin' around and give you a call."

Steele turned his attention toward the campsite. A red tent was collapsed in a heap, and the ground around it was littered with strewn garments, food, and trash. Walking closer, the sheriff could tell the tent had been shredded by something sharp. Carl followed his boss and examined the devastation.

The deputy shook his head, visibly uncomfortable. "I don't like this, Sheriff. I sure hope we don't have ourselves a killer running around town."

"Looks too much like a murder for me to think anything otherwise. Apparently ol' Sully picked the right time to be on vacation." Mayor Sully Vargas took a two-week vacation every year with his family, and right now the Vargas family was on a Mediterranean cruise. It would do little good to call the mayor. Even if the sheriff could reach him by phone, the cruise ship would keep him at sea too long for the mayor to get back here any sooner than expected. As acting town authority, Sheriff Steele would have to make all the decisions affecting this investigation. He did not want to make any mistakes.

"Run back to the station and get the kit," the sheriff directed. "We're gonna need to scour the scene, dust everything we can for prints, take photos, take samples... the whole nine yards."

Deputy Riggins sighed. His day had just turned into a long evening. But he knew it was what they needed to do. "You got it, Sheriff."

"And get ol' Lewis to start callin' around to see if he can locate Walt Jr. Or anyone who knows where he is."

"Okay," said Carl. Then he turned and swiftly walked the trail back to the cruiser.

Sheriff Steele informed Donnie Broden and his friends that they could leave the scene. Then, after thanking them and watching them depart, he turned his eyes back to the mayhem of the campsite.

The tent was destroyed, as was the fiberglass cooler lying near the fire pit. Mangled cans and packages of food were left nearby. Pieces of shredded sleeping bags and clothing were everywhere. It almost looked like a wild animal attack.

But wild animals don't break into trucks and pull people out, he mused.

Figuring he had better let his wife know he would be working late, the sheriff grabbed his phone. At that moment he saw a notification stating he had a new voice message. He connected to his voicemail and listened. It was Marty, saying that he had found something very interesting in the waters of Pirate's Bend.

The sheriff, hoping to hear Marty tell him he figured out what had happened to Earl Goates, eagerly returned the diver's call.

"Hey, Sheriff," Marty greeted when he picked up. "Where are you?"

"Hey, Marty. I'm up here past Pirate's Point, checking out an incident. Are you nearby at the cove?"

"No, I'm actually in town. Came by the station to see you, Deputy Simkins told me you were out."

Sheriff Steele cut to the chase. "So what did you find in the cove? A body, I hope."

"No body, I'm afraid," said Marty. "But maybe a little more information about where that claw came from."

"I'm all ears."

"It's a lot. Listen, why don't we meet back at the station, and I'll tell you everything in person."

"Okay, Marty. As soon as Spud gets back here to take over, I'll take the car to the station."

"I'll meet you there in a little bit then."

"Sounds good." Steele ended the call. Then he dialed home and informed his wife of the situation. Afterward, he resumed his search for clues at the campsite.

Deputy Riggins returned a short time later with the crime scene analysis kit. Sheriff Steele instructed him to cover the job thoroughly, announced that he was taking the car back to meet with Marty, and that he would be back as soon as possible to help the deputy finish up. Then the sheriff headed into town to hear what news his diver had for him.

Steele pulled to the curb in front of the station and parked. Marty was standing outside the building, waiting by the door. He nodded to Marty as he walked to the entrance. "Hey, buddy. C'mon, let's go inside."

The sheriff opened the door, escorting Marty inside. Behind the front desk sat Lewis Simkins, a long-time Sweetboro policeman. He was black, in his late fifties, and usually worked the night shift at the station. It was quiet and for the most part peaceful, usually consisting of him sipping coffee and watching DVDs while manning the station. It was the perfect shift for Lewis to spend his few remaining years on the force working.

"Evening, Sheriff," he greeted. "Marty."

The two men nodded to Lewis and continued through the station to the sheriff's office. There they each took a seat on opposite sides of the desk.

"Alright, Marty," said Steele, "what did you find?"

"Okay," the diver began. "I did a thorough search in the water along the shoreline where the boat was found. But I saw nothing indicating any presence of marine life larger than feeder fish."

"And still no body."

"No body. And I seriously doubt we're going to find one at this point. I think we would've by now." Marty shifted in his seat. "But check this out. I found an underwater entrance to a cave system. And guess where it leads?"

The sheriff wanted very much to respond with something witty like 'the end of this story', but he chose to stay serious. "Where?"

"There's a big cavern below Pirate's Point. Very dark, except for a tiny bit of light coming down through the hole at Pirate's

Point. I was able to get out of the water and walk around in there. I saw what looked like a nesting area, although I don't know for what kind of animal. And then I found a small pool with a bunch of what looked like eggs inside."

"*Eggs?*"

"Well, that's what they looked like. For all I know they could be geodes, or just smoothed rocks or coral."

"But you saw a nest?"

"More like a den. Seaweed and kelp had been layered in one single corner, and nowhere else in the cavern. I think it was placed there by an animal. And I *did* hear some kind of animal in there."

The sheriff leaned forward. "Yeah?"

"Yes, more than one. I think they realized I was there and started to converge on me. I didn't know if they were gators, or wildcats, or what; I just knew I was not in a good situation. I jumped back in the water and swam out through the cave."

"Did you get one of those eggs?"

Marty hung his head. "No, dammit. I intended on taking one, although I wasn't sure how I'd carry it with my flashlight, or if it was even something safe to touch. But when I heard those things moving in, my only thought was to get the hell out of there."

"Understandable." The sheriff tilted his chair back on its rear legs. "It's a shame, though, I'da loved to see what they are, eggs or minerals or what-have-you."

"Me too," Marty agreed. "I just may have to go back in there and try again. But I'll bring a weapon next time, something a little more powerful than a dive knife. Just in case."

"Well, we still don't have anything helping us with the investigation of Earl's disappearance. Although whatever you heard in the cave might've had something to do with it." Steele leaned forward, the chair legs returning flat to the floor. "But we still have no body."

"Nope. But it's not for lack of looking."

"True. Thank you, Marty, for searching at least. I'm gonna have to close the investigation, pending any further information. For now I'll just have to say poor old Earl was the victim of an animal attack, based on the condition of his boat and the blood found, with no body recovered."

Marty nodded. "That's what I'd go with."

The sheriff stroked his bushy mustache. "In the meantime, I suppose, it might be a good idea to put some signs up to keep people out of Pirate's Bend."

CHAPTER 12

The moon looked misty through the bottom of the upturned glass. Cinch let the last of the moonshine run into his mouth, swallowed it, and returned the glass to its coaster on the patio table. Smacking his lips, the old Creole looked around the porch for his bottle. He located it on the planks near his chair and reached for it to pour himself another glass.

A splash was heard in the dark distance, in the water at the edge of his property. Fish jumping for mosquitoes, he figured, since the time was right for evening feeding. There were some big fish in the inlet that bordered his back yard. He had caught bass, crappie, and bream in there. Farther down the water a bit, in the estuary, red drum and spotted seatrout were the prominent inhabitants.

Suddenly Cinch felt the urge to go fishing. Sure, he was drunk, but so what? He did not have to work tomorrow, and he was certainly no stranger to fishing while inebriated. He loved being by the water at night, especially with a bottle of his homemade booze, and he loved the pull of a defiant fish on his hook even more.

With a mellow smile forming on his face, he pushed himself up from his chair. Then, staggering a little, he walked inside his house to gather his gear. He collected his fishing pole, flashlight, and wading boots. He inspected his pole, making sure his favorite lure was still tied to the end of the line, slipped his boots on, and then made his way back outside to the porch.

Grabbing his bottle of hooch, the contented old man turned the flashlight on and hobbled off the porch and down through the trees toward the nearby inlet. Three minutes later he arrived at the water's edge. The fresh water glistened in the moonlight when he got there, welcoming him to a night of pleasant fishing.

Cinch set down his bottle and wedged the flashlight under his arm. Then, with his hands free, he set up for his first cast. Making sure he could clear the overhead tree branches, he cast his lure out. It plopped into the water, and Cinch sat before shutting off the flashlight and slowly reeling his bait in.

After a few casts, he paused to take a pull from his bottle. The alcohol warmed his throat and belly nicely. Then he resumed casting out his lure and bringing it back in.

Nothing was biting. Cinch frowned; maybe he wasn't going to get whatever made that splash here a while ago. But he might catch something farther downshore. With hopes of finding better sport in the estuary, he turned his flashlight back on and moved down the inlet.

He had to duck underneath the sheets of Spanish moss draping down from the limbs of the waterside oaks. The soft plants grazed and tickled his head as he passed beneath. Cinch walked fifty yards before he was at the salt marsh.

Here the fresh water met the salt water coming in from the Atlantic. Tufts of smooth cordgrass crowded the surface, which would not accommodate Cinch's lure fishing. He went a little farther, until he found an open bank of pluff mud. The distinct odor found its way into his nose when he stepped closer, the sulfuric smell of decay that was indicative of salt marsh mud. The pluff mud was a great spot for harvesting oysters, and sometimes blue crab, but that was not Cinch's goal tonight. He would wade out into the water, past the boot-gripping muck, until his feet could find a firm sandy spot. Then he would be in a good position for catching some red drum or flounder worth bringing home.

He readied his pole, pocketed his bottle and flashlight, and began plodding through the mud and into the water. About ten feet from shore, while the water still was shallow enough to stay out of his high wading boots, he found a sandy area that felt right for stable standing. Cinch cast his lure out from there, and he saw the ripples it produced in the moon's reflection.

After another swig of his shine, Cinch almost lost his balance. It was a good thing he was out beyond the squishy mud, or he would have fallen for sure. He was getting pretty drunk. Shrugging, he re-established his underwater footing and took another drink.

Just then a foul smell hit his nose, stronger and more distinct than the odor from the pluff mud. It was more like rotten eggs.

Confused by this foreign scent, Cinch squinted his eyes and looked around in the dark.

On the shoreline thirty yards down from him, a shape moved in the cordgrass. Focusing on the shape under the faint light of the moon, Cinch held his pole under his arm and reached for his flashlight. He turned the light on and aimed it down the shore toward the ocean. He caught a glimpse of something unbelievable just before it slipped into the water and out of sight.

Cinch froze for a minute, his mind processing what he had just seen. It instantly triggered memories from his Louisiana childhood, many years ago. He recalled the vivid nightmares his Creole grandmother used to give him by telling stories of ancient, aquatic monsters that would come for children if they misbehaved. And those images in his head from long ago looked very much like what he thought he just saw.

An uncomfortable chill washed down his body, and he trembled. Something horrible was out there in the water, something evil. Keeping his flashlight fixed at the spot, he saw faint ripples created by motion under the water.

And whatever was causing them was moving in his direction.

Cinch decided he needed to get the hell out of there. Holding his pole and flashlight, he turned around and quickly headed for the shore. His feet found the mud again, which gripped and pulled his boots while he tried to hurry through the water. He fought the pluff mud, his leg muscles working hard to lift his boots from each step, and anxiety was beginning to take him.

Nervously, he shined the light once more at the water downstream to see if the threat was still there. The ripples appeared again, then again, drawing closer.

Cinch's anxiety was now absolute panic. One of the monsters of his childhood nightmares was almost upon him. Terrified, he pulled with his legs until he had made it through the mud and finally to shore.

He ran from the area. Following the shoreline upstream, he rushed back the way he came, back toward the inlet and his house. Within moments he heard splashing from where he just was, something getting out of the water. His heart pounding, he tried to run even faster.

Being drunk did not help his situation; he started to feel light-headed from the vigorous exercise he had unexpectedly forced upon his body. His legs began to go numb. He prayed they would not cramp up and stop his flight. Hearing the rustling sounds of something else moving behind him, his fear and adrenaline kicked in to keep his legs churning. He looked straight ahead while dashing through the oaks and Spanish moss. He kept going, hoping he would not trip on a root or run into an outstretched limb. After a minute, he no longer heard anything pursuing him. But he kept running as fast as his legs would allow.

Cinch finally arrived at his property. He scurried up the slope to his house and scampered up the steps to his back porch. His pole and flashlight were no longer with him; he had no idea where he had dropped them, nor did he care. All that mattered to him was getting inside the house and hiding from the monster. He hurried inside through the sliding glass door, latching it behind him.

He quickly went through the house to make sure each and every one of his doors and windows were shut and locked. Then he turned the lights off and tiptoed to his bedroom, where he crawled into bed and did not make a sound.

CHAPTER 13

Ricky Young sat at the breakfast table, smoking a Marlboro, quietly watching his son in the kitchen. It was another lovely day outside, and Ricky had plans to enjoy it to the full. But he could not make his secret rendezvous happen until after Danny left the house. So he sat, patiently, and tried to coax Danny to leave.

"Nice day out," said Ricky, "you really should go enjoy it before it gets too hot."

Danny stopped putting up the dishes and peered out the window to take notice. "It is nice out. Don't know what I'd do, though."

Ricky was quick to reply. "Go look for a job." Then, realizing this option was not one that would lure his son away, he added, "Or go fishing with your friends. Or hiking. Just take advantage of this good weather."

Confused, Danny raised an eyebrow. Usually his father burdened him with chores, punishment for not being employed. "Are you sure?"

Ricky nodded, taking a drag of his cigarette. "Yeah, go on out and enjoy. Before you know it, summer will be gone and it'll start getting cold out."

"Okay." Danny finished with the dishes and rinsed the sink. Then he dried his hands with the dishtowel and glanced at the phone on the wall. "Maybe I'll give Hannah a call and she if she wants to do something."

Ricky grimaced a bit, squinting his eyes. "Hannah Dermont? I don't know, son… I'm afraid she's out of your league."

Danny frowned. "What do you mean?"

"She's too good for you, boy. You need to set your sights on someone more realistic."

"Thanks for the support, Dad."

"Look, you've been trying at her for years and never got anywhere. Don't you think it's time you gave up and started looking for other options?"

The son shrugged. "I suppose. I'm crazy about her though." His mind conjured the image of her hearty blonde hair, sparkling blue eyes, and perfect body.

Ricky shooed the air with his hand. "Stop wasting your time. There's plenty of fish in the sea that can make you happy."

As much as he hated admitting it, his father was right. Hannah had always managed to keep Danny at a distance, warding off his advances time and time again. And there were endless other young women out there to be found. "I suppose," Danny repeated.

"There ya go. Now go on, get outta here, go do something fun. I gotta focus on work stuff here today."

Danny needed no further convincing. He squeezed his feet into his sneakers, took bug spray and sunscreen from the cabinet, and said goodbye to his oddly-agreeable father. Then he left the house, strolling across the lawn toward the forest.

Ricky watched through the kitchen window until his son disappeared into the trees beyond the yard.

Then he picked up his cell phone and dialed his young employee, Hannah Dermont.

"Hey, you," she said warmly when she picked up. "I was just layin' here thinkin' about you."

Her sultry tone made his groin tingle a little as he imagined her sprawled across her bed wearing nothing but a naughty smile. "Hey, pumpkin," he said. "Ready to go?"

"I sure am. You coming to pick me up?"

"No," he replied, "can't have your mother knowing about us, you know that."

"Fine," said Hannah. "But I'm gonna need some gas money. I'm almost empty."

"I gotcha covered."

"Thanks, baby. Meet you at the store, then?"

"Yeah, that's what I was thinking. Pick you up around back, usual spot."

"Usual spot," she confirmed.

"I'll be there in twenty."

Ricky hung up and trotted upstairs to get ready for her. Looking at his reflection in the bathroom mirror, he smiled slyly to himself. For a man of forty-five, he had it going on. He was still relatively handsome, even with the gray mixed into the brown of his goatee, in good physical shape, financially independent, and having sex with a beautiful girl less than half his age. *Yes sir*, he thought while running a little gel through his hair, *you da man*.

Sometimes he felt bad for having a secret relationship with the object of his own son's desire, but most of the time he just felt like a winner who acquired a prize most men his age never get. One of the perks of owning his own grocery store, he justified, was that he deserved to get his hands on any hot, young employee he could win over. And Hannah was just that.

He had been sleeping with her for about a month now. She was not the first youthful employee he had been secretly intimate with, and probably would not be the last. But for now, she was his.

Ricky grabbed a heavy quilt and made his way back downstairs to the kitchen. There he added a couple of bottles of wine to his pile. Then he hopped into his F-350 pickup, lit a cigarette, and headed into town.

Five minutes later he was at his grocery store. Cruising slowly, he pulled around to the back of the store to look for Hannah's car. Sure enough, her second-hand Impala was parked next to the loading dock. After ensuring nobody else was around to witness them being together, he parked next to her on the right.

Hannah grabbed her purse, stepped out of her vehicle, and sauntered around the front of her car. As she approached the truck, Ricky took note of how sexy she looked today. Her blonde hair – just long enough to graze her shoulders – bounced and gleamed in the summer sun, a bit of mascara framed her bright blue eyes, and the cutoff jean shorts hugged her hips nicely.

"Hey, you," said Hannah when she opened the passenger door and hopped aboard. Then she leaned over to kiss him.

Ricky kissed her back, tasting cherry lip balm. "Hey, pumpkin. You look especially hot today."

"Thank you," she grinned. "Just for you." She buckled her seatbelt and released a quiet sigh. "Gimme a smoke, will ya?"

"Yeah, sure." Ricky handed her his Marlboros from the dash, and she pulled one from the pack. He lit it for her, then put the truck in gear and began driving back around to the front of his store.

Glancing around, Ricky saw nobody outside to recognize him. Satisfied that Hannah had not been seen in the vehicle with him, he pulled onto Main Street and headed toward the northern hills. He would drive the backroads to their destination in order to avoid the noticing eyes of other motorists.

Cruising along the wooded dirt road, Hannah was quiet. Ricky noticed a distracted look on her face. "Are you okay?" he asked. "You look like something's bothering you."

"Cappy was out all night last night, and he hasn't come back today either. He's never been gone this long."

Ricky, who despised cats, fought to refrain from saying anything derogatory about Captain Purrbucket. "I'm sure he'll turn up," was all he could say.

"I hope so."

"He will, pumpkin." Ricky set a reassuring hand on her leg. "I'm sure of it. That's just what cats do." He had no idea what cats really did, as he had never lived with one. As far as he knew, cats could only shit, lick, bite, and scratch. But he needed to cheer up his partner if he was going to make the most of their excursion. "He'll be back by the time you get home. Now come on, don't give it another thought. We're gonna have a nice day together."

Hannah smiled at Ricky's response. One of the things she liked about him was his ability to take control of any situation and make it better. Ever since she began working for him at the grocery store she took note of his take-charge, everything's-under-control manner. Sure, he was strict and callous at times, but never to her. He had always treated her different, special.

At first Hannah wasn't sure how she felt about Ricky being so much older than her, but his flirting brought forth her curiosity. After all, he was attractive, mature, had money, and knew what he wanted. And once she submitted to going to bed with him, she discovered he was also very good at pleasing a woman. Nobody had ever brought her to orgasm like Ricky could.

As the weeks went on, she began falling in love with him. She dared not tell him that, though, at least not yet. She didn't want to risk scaring him away. But today, while on their quiet drive to the coast, she thought she should at least test the waters.

"Wouldn't it be nice if we didn't have to sneak around like we do? If we could stop hiding, and come and go as we please together?"

Ricky turned to her, raising an eyebrow. *Oh shit*, he thought, *here it comes*. He had worried the time would come when she would become too attached and want a public relationship with him. But that would be a problem for him, since Hannah was nothing more than some hot, young thing that he was just using for sex. And he would replace her someday with the next sexy, young employee that took a fancy to him.

"I think we're doing just fine like we are," he replied. "No one else needs to know."

"Why not? We're both adults, what does it matter if people know we're together?"

"The town would definitely frown upon it, what with the big age difference between us. You're going to the same community college as my son, for Chrissake!" *That, and I just don't see myself wanting to be with you forever*, he added mentally.

"Why do we care about what they think?"

Ricky fidgeted. "Well, for one thing, people might stop shopping at my store. They'd turn their noses up on us and buy all their groceries across the street. That would ruin me, pumpkin."

Hannah let that logic settle in. As much as she wanted to be with Ricky, she realized they would be outcasts, the store would go under, and Ricky would soon have no money left to support them. She sighed. "I guess you're right."

"Sure I am, pumpkin. We just have to keep things our little secret, like we have been."

Ricky followed the country road to the coast. He passed Pirate's Bend and continued north until the road ended at a rocky beach. He parked the truck on the edge of the dirt cul-de-sac, turned the motor off, and grinned to his companion.

"Let's go, pumpkin."

Hannah was excited. She knew where he was taking her, and it was one of her favorite spots. The rocky coast here was fed by a quiet river that was hardly ever visited. She and Ricky had discovered a beautiful, secluded spot several weeks ago. It was upriver a ways, through the thicket of oaks and pines, where they would never be disturbed.

Grabbing the quilt and the wine, Ricky led Hannah down to the mouth of the river. She shouldered her purse and trailed him along the edge to where the trees created a barrier. The couple crouched and worked their way through the branches until they reached the clearer setting beyond. Then they followed the river upstream, past where the salt water from below mixed with the fresh water, until they found their private spot.

There was a gentle slope of long grass between the water and a large oak. Ricky walked beneath the hearty branches, unfurled the quilt, and spread it over the grass. Then he and Hannah sat, hearing only the sounds of soothing birdsong and the burbling of the easy river. While Ricky opened one of the wine bottles, Hannah tilted her head back, admiring the outstretched Spanish moss dangling over them.

Ricky wasted no time. He felt especially horny today, and wanted to get her in the same mood. He leaned in and rested his mouth on her exposed neck. A murmur of agreement left her lips as he softly kissed and nibbled.

He moved his lips up to hers. She met his kisses enthusiastically, pulling him close. Then she grabbed his shirt and lifted it off of him. Smiling to his lover, Ricky sat back and unbuckled his belt. Hannah peeled her own shirt off and undid her bra to bare her breasts, pink nipples perking.

Ricky could feel himself hardening. The lovely young vision before him was everything he longed to have today. His smile curling to one side, Ricky unbuttoned her cutoffs and pulled them slowly down her legs. Then he slid her teal panties down the same way, brought his face between her legs, and kissed the nakedness he exposed.

"Dirty old man," she purred.

"You got that right."

Ricky began to kiss and lick his partner, slowly at first. As his passion and vigor increased, Hannah squirmed ecstatically under his tongue. She was very thankful for her experienced lover; he certainly knew his way around a woman's body.

There was a sudden rustling of leaves nearby.

Hannah stiffened nervously, sitting up. "What was that?"

Ricky had heard it too. "Probably just a deer," he assured. "Relax, pumpkin, there's no one here except us and the critters.

And they certainly don't want anything to do with being around us."

Hannah studied their surroundings for a moment, then determined nobody was there. She relaxed again, and lay back down on the quilt.

That's it, thought Ricky, *just lie back and give me that sweet, young pussy*. He resumed his oral performance. She was now very wet, and he was getting very hard.

He heard the rustling leaves again, causing him to pause his tongue. And he detected a new, unpleasant odor in the air.

Something grabbed him hard by the ankle and ripped him away from Hannah. He suddenly found himself being dragged rapidly down the slope to the river. He heard Hannah's horrified voice screaming his name just before he was pulled under the water.

Confused and shocked, Ricky struggled to assess what had happened. Then he imagined an alligator taking him into the river, and he realized the danger he could be in. Wildly, desperately, he fought his way to the surface.

He emerged and drew a deep breath of air. When the water flowed out of his eyes, Ricky was able to see Hannah on the river's edge, flailing and screaming. And he saw something on her.

At first he thought it was an alligator, but he quickly realized the dark, olive-green thing was something else entirely. The man-sized thing had her in its arms – its *tentacles* – and was biting her. Hannah was shrieking hysterically, her eyes wide and rolling. Blood was flowing quickly from her shoulder, covering her breasts and belly. Ricky saw the tentacles rip into her flesh with what looked like talons at the tips. Then he was pulled under once more.

Ricky felt something unbelievably strong wrap around his torso and squeeze. Terror and dread consumed him as he realized what had just happened to Hannah was happening to him. He struggled with all his might, but could not free himself from his attacker. He felt his body ripped open and pieces being torn away.

As blood and air left Ricky's body, so did consciousness and life.

CHAPTER 14

Mason awoke to a chill in the morning air. He opened his eyes and focused them on the bedroom window. It had been open since last night, letting the evening air into the room to help cool the house. But this morning had not brought with it the warmth of the sun. Instead it was gray, gloomy, and breezy.

Shuffling to the window, Mason gazed at the skies beyond. He got to the window, closed it, and studied the scene outside. Clouds were building, blowing inward from the sea; a storm was coming in.

This would be a good day for Mason to stay in and clean the house. It had not been tended to for over a week, and could surely use some dusting, sweeping, and vacuuming. But first he wanted some coffee time.

Mason threw on a bathrobe and went downstairs to the kitchen. After starting a pot of coffee, he ventured to the front porch to grab the daily newspaper. The breeze from the looming clouds brought leaves from the trees scuttling across the wooden porch. He watched them skip past his feet and disappear over the side.

He returned to the kitchen, poured a mug of coffee, and sat at the table with his paper. Two hours softly went by while Mason enjoyed the printed pieces and refills of steaming coffee. For the first time since the death of his mother, he began to feel comfortable as the new master of his home.

Inevitably it was time to clean. Mason set his mug in the sink and searched the cabinet below for cleaning supplies. He found the bathroom cleaner, scrubber, glass cleaner, paper towels, and furniture polish, setting them on the counter one at a time. Then he collected the mass into his arms and went upstairs to begin.

After scrubbing and wiping down the bathrooms, he needed a break. He had not yet eaten, and his stomach was making him well aware of the fact. Looking at a clock in the bedroom, he noticed it was noon. Sherrie's Shack would be open now, and a hot, hearty lunch was just what he needed.

Mason arrived at the restaurant five minutes later. He parked his old Mazda and walked to the entrance, but then frowned when he saw a sign on the door stating the eatery was temporarily closed. Seeing movement through the windows, he tried the door. It was unlocked, so Mason went inside.

He saw Eaver, her hair pulled back and held with a clip, bringing broken boards in from the back and adding them to the stack on the counter. She looked upset.

"Hey, Eave," said Mason. "What's going on?"

Eaver sighed. "The smokehouse is destroyed. It's a wreck back there."

"What? What happened?"

"Not sure, probably animals. All the meat's gone."

"Shit. That sucks."

"C'mon back," she said, "we could use a hand."

"Sure." Mason followed his friend through the kitchen and outside to where the smokehouse was kept. He was shocked by what he saw.

The structure no longer existed. Three of the four walls were gone, reduced to scraps of broken cedar that were scattered all over. The gabled roof had fallen and was leaning on the corner of the brick firebox. Cinch was pushing the roof to the side so he could retrieve more debris from the ground. Sherrie was there too, helping clean up the wreckage.

"Hi Mason," said Sherrie when she saw him. "Can you believe this?"

"No," he replied. "This is crazy. Like a tornado hit it." There was a hint of rotten egg stench in the air, and Mason winced. "What's that smell from?"

"Dunno," Sherrie shrugged. "It seems to be on some of the busted wood."

"Smells like sulfur."

"De smell of hellfire an' brimstone," said Cinch, standing straight to address Mason. "It's de sliggers."

Mason blinked. "What?"

"He's been goin' on about monsters from the deep," said

Eaver, with a slight roll of her eyes.

"I *saw* 'em," the old cook insisted. "De other night, when I be fishin'. And dey smell like dat, like rotten egg. And now dey come here, last night, for my meats."

Indeed, hardly any of the meat normally held in the smokehouse was anywhere to be seen. Just a few bones and bits and pieces of pork spotting the area. "We don't have bears around here," Mason stated. "I wonder what could've done this."

"Could it have been gators?" offered Sherrie.

"No ma'am, dees is *sliggers*."

Mason's curiosity was piqued. "What's a sligger?" he asked the cook.

"Monsters from de pits of Hell. My granny done told me 'bout dem long ago, when I's just a child, but I remember de stories like yesterday. She used to say dey was part devil, part man, part animal. Wit' teeth like a shark, tentacles like a squid, claws like a gator. Dey come up from de water to take bad children to de underworld."

"Sounds like the bogeyman," Mason said with half a smile.

"De bogeyman o' de water," nodded the cook.

"Sounds terrifying," said Eaver, a twinge of uneasiness in her voice. She gazed over her shoulder at the nearby coast below. "Why would your granny even *tell* you stories like that?"

"As fascinating as your Louisiana children's stories are," Sherrie interjected, "I'm sure something else is responsible for what happened here last night."

"I tell you, I saw 'em de other night. An' I smelled dat smell of brimstone with 'em. Same smell dey left here in de smokehouse. We got sliggers, for sure."

Sherrie shook her head. "I'd put my money on wildcats or gators before I'd blame any 'bogeymen from the deep'."

Cinch shrugged. "Say what you want. I know what I know." He continued clearing the destruction to make room for him to begin reconstructing the smokehouse.

"Holy shit," said Danny Young, who had found his way around the restaurant to where the others' voices had led him. They turned their heads to him when they heard his voice.

"Hey, Danny," Mason acknowledged. "How's it goin'?"

Surveying the area around what used to be the smokehouse,

Danny just shook his head. "What happened here?"

"We're not sure," said Sherrie, "some kind of animal, we figure."

"Got dat right," Cinch declared. "Some *bad* animal."

Danny was concerned about what had happened to Sherrie's restaurant, but something else was already on his mind today. "Hey, you guys haven't seen my dad anywhere, have you?"

Sherrie looked up. "Ricky? No, hon. Haven't seen him in a while. Why, is something wrong?"

"Well, no, it's just that he wasn't there when I came home yesterday and he hasn't been home since. He didn't leave a note or anything, which is unusual. He's not at the store, and not answering his phone either. I left a couple messages."

"Huh," said Eaver. "That doesn't sound like him. Although you should probably be happy having some time without him bitchin' at you."

"Yeah," Mason seconded, "don't look a gift horse in the mouth."

"That's not nice, kids," Sherrie scolded softly. But even she agreed that a day without the unpleasant, arrogant Ricky Young was a nice thing.

Just then the rain began to fall. The storm front had arrived, throwing colder air and moisture at the coastal town.

Sherrie stood. "C'mon, kids, I'll make y'all some lunch. And then I suppose I should open up the restaurant." She led the group through the back door and into the kitchen.

Cinch, not hungry, stayed behind. The strong odor on the wood reminded him of his frightening ordeal two nights ago, and it killed his appetite. He remained outside, in the gentle rain, to continue rebuilding the smokehouse as best he could.

CHAPTER 15

"Where the fuck is he?"

Mitch Haverson and Jesse Reed looked at each other, shrugged, and turned their heads back to Malcolm Gibbs, who was sitting opposite them in the diner's booth.

Big Mal clenched his phone angrily in frustration. He had not been able to get hold of his friend Walt Echerson for four days now. And they had marijuana plants to tend to, selling to be done. Mal addressed his co-workers. "Has he called you guys?"

"No, Mal," said Jesse. "Haven't heard from him."

"It's like he just disappeared, dude," added Mitch, the concern in his voice equal to that of his leader's.

Was that little bitch right? Mal wondered. *Did Walt actually decide to leave the group, like Eaver said?* Her snotty remark had angered him the other day, and was still eating at him. Partially because deep down, he had always wanted Eaver – at least since her boobs began developing nicely in high school – but she had never given him the time of day. Instead, she spent all her time with that twerp Mason. "Fuckin' Eaver," he mumbled, reaching for a french fry.

Jesse heard him. "Huh?"

"Remember what she said the other day when we ran into her and Red? About how maybe Walt decided to leave?"

"He wouldn't do that," Mitch snorted. "He makes good money with us, and he's seein' that little hottie Sarah Primley. Why the hell would he leave all that?"

"Good point," said Mal. The crew did indeed make good money growing and selling marijuana, although it came with the risk of getting caught. But they were careful about who they sold to. The gang mostly sold in outlying towns, directly to local dealers with whom they had established trust. And the few customers they had here in town would never dare turn them in,

69

because Mal's crew knew where they all lived. The Sweetboro Boys had a system that was running smoothly, successfully.

"She was just fucking with you, being a bitch," Jesse added. "I'm sure Walt's shacked up with Sarah somewhere, tappin' that ass. Eaver don't know what she's talking about."

Mal nodded. "That's for sure. I mean, all she does is spend time with her mom. And fuckin' Mason. I don't know why she hangs out with Red." He snarled as his mind conjured an image of Mason smiling cheesily. "That little runt always thought he was better than us. Smug fuckin' college boy."

Jesse pulled his phone out. "Still, Walt should've let us know where he's at." He tried to call their friend one more time. After a moment he shook his head. "Just goes to his voicemail."

Big Mal grunted uneasily. Then he grabbed another fry and continued to eat his lunch. His buddies quietly did the same.

It was still raining when they emerged from the diner. The rainfall was light, just a drizzle, but would worsen throughout the day and into the night. The crew hastened to Mal's covered Jeep and jumped inside. They had work to do today, money to make, and the weather was not going to get any better. Mal figured the sooner they got started, the sooner they could be finished.

It would take less time if Walt was here to help, Mal brooded.

Then he had a scary thought. He turned to his cohorts. "You don't suppose he did something stupid and got arrested, do ya?"

"I can't imagine so," said Jesse. "And besides, couldn't he still call us from jail?"

"Unless he only got one phone call and needed to call a lawyer or something," Mal pointed out.

"Maybe you should call the police and see if he's there," Mitch suggested.

Mal pondered the idea of Walt getting busted for selling pot. If he had, the police would likely have learned of the group's operation and picked up Mal and the others by now, which had obviously not happened. *So no*, thought Mal, *Walt's probably not in jail*.

Still, calling the police was not a bad idea. Maybe they knew something about where Walt was. Mal decided to call the station.

The phone rang at the front desk of the police station, and Carl Riggins was there to pick up. "Sheriff's office," he said into the mouthpiece. "Deputy Riggins speaking."

"Um, hi there. This is Mal. Mal Gibbs. I was wondering if you could help me with something."

"Hello, Malcolm," said Carl, recognizing the voice of the local young man. "I'm glad you called, actually. We've been trying to get hold of you."

Mal tensed; it was never good for a drug dealer to have the police looking for him. "Yeah? Why's that?"

"We found Walt Jr.'s truck abandoned, day before last. But no trace of young Walt. Just a mess of a campground, and damage to his truck."

"Really?" Mal said, turning to his friends and raising his eyebrow. "Where?"

"Up past Pirate's Point, overlooking the coast. We've been trying to locate Walt ever since, with no luck yet. You're one of his friends, so we were hoping maybe you'd know where he is? Or if you can think of any of his other friends that might know?"

Mal shook his head without realizing it. "No," he said into the phone. "That's actually why I was callin' you. Was wonderin' if maybe you knew where he was, or if he was in trouble or something. We haven't heard from him in a few days."

"Well, do us a favor, will ya? If you hear from him, have him get in touch with us. We'll keep his truck here at the station in the meantime. Okay?"

"Okay, will do," said Mal. Then he ended the call and turned to his buddies. "Cops don't know where he is, which I guess is good. Means nothing bad happened. Except…"

"Except what?" Mitch asked.

"They found Walt's truck by Pirate's Point. Said it was damaged, and the campground was a mess too."

Jesse grinned. "I bet he took Sarah camping, for a night alone with her."

Mal restated his earlier question. "But where the fuck is he *now?*"

"Something could've happened to them," Mitch offered.

"Like what?"

Mitch simply shrugged. "I guess we'll find out when we see him again."

That would have to be the answer for now. With or without Walt, the crew had work to do. "Well, let's get a move on. Sooner we unload our stuff, sooner we can get back." Mal started the Jeep and drove off in the rain.

They spent the next few hours cruising the outlying towns that were about forty-five minutes away from Sweetboro. Their fellow dealers met with them, bought their marijuana, and agreed on the next transaction date. When all the pot was sold, Mal started the wet drive home.

Before calling it a day, Mal would make a stop at the greenhouse. They had not been there in a couple of days, and it was time to tend to the plants. New sprouts would be added to the line and the others moved down until the mature plants at the end would come down to be picked.

It was getting dark by the time the group arrived at their secluded greenhouse. As Mal rounded the last corner up the hill, his headlights illuminated a shocking sight.

The greenhouse was destroyed. The roof was still up, barely, but one of the walls looked like it had been peeled off by a backhoe. The gaping opening revealed the carnage inside. Water pipes and fluorescent grow lights were awkwardly strewn among the greenery.

"What the fuck!" Mal exclaimed. "What the goddamn *fuck!*" He skidded the Jeep to a halt. Then he and his partners rushed out to investigate.

The structure was barely standing. Mal felt the hot flush of rage surge through him as he contemplated the amount of money this catastrophe would likely cost him. He made his way to the greenhouse, the others at his heels, and tentatively stepped inside through the damaged side.

The partition walls were ripped down, which had brought down the drip system that continually dispensed a mix of water and fertilizer. Sections of PVC pipe were strewn about. The fluorescent grow lights were down as well, leaving broken bulb glass on the plants and ground.

Surprisingly, and to the relief of the owners, the plants themselves had not been harmed. Mal studied each plant like a concerned parent.

"The plants are okay," he said. "And it looks like they're all still here."

"The breaker box is intact," Mitch reported. "Whoever came in here just fucked with the lights and fan system."

"And the watering system," said Jesse. "We're gonna have to repair all of it, which is gonna suck."

"Somebody really did a number on us," Mal growled.

Baffled, Mitch asked, "But why would they leave the plants?"

"I dunno," shrugged Mal. "Probably knew that they'd be signing their own death warrants if they went so far as taking our plants."

Jesse attempted to focus on the positives. "Well at least we still have all our pot, so that's great news. All we have to do is fix the greenhouse."

Nothing was going to change Mal's foul mood. "That's gonna cost money," he growled. "And we gotta get the watering system put back together and running again, and right now. I'm not gonna risk losing any of our plants."

Mitch went to the ground and began gathering the pieces of pipe.

"And that *fucking smell!*" Mal exclaimed. "Like rotten eggs!"

"That's sulfur, dude," Mitch claimed.

"Who the fuck would have sulfur?"

"I dunno. A college boy?"

CHAPTER 16

"Go on, Cinch, get outta here."

The cook shook his head. "I still gotta clean de kitchen, Miss Eaver."

"Nonsense," Eaver shooed. "You darn near worked yourself to death fixing up the smokehouse. Now please, go home. Mason and I can handle the kitchen."

Cinch had done an inordinate amount of work clearing and rebuilding today, and the fatigue he was feeling showed on his aged face. He looked to Mason, who nodded his assurance. "Okay, Miss Eaver," said Cinch, grateful for the relief. "Thank you. I see you tomorrow, den."

It had been a long day at Sherrie's Shack. Cinch had spent the majority of the day patching up the smokehouse, while Sherrie took over cooking duties in the kitchen. Thankfully there were not many customers today, with the dreary weather, and Sherrie had no trouble handling the orders. Sherrie had gone home fifteen minutes ago, just after the restaurant closed, and now Eaver was sending a weary Cinch home to rest.

When the old Creole left, Eaver closed the door behind him and turned to face Mason. "I'm worried about that old boy," she said.

Mason was concerned as well. "You mean that talk about the sligger monsters?"

"Yeah. I think he really believes what he was saying."

"Think his age is starting to affect his mind?"

"I dunno, he *is* getting up there in age. But despite that, I'm sure his grandmother did tell him those stories."

"Well sure," reasoned Mason, "but probably something they used to say down there to make kids behave. Like when we were told about Santa."

Eaver grinned. "I suppose. And he was probably drunk as a skunk the other night when he said he saw them. Some kind of critter by the water, his age, booze, and his imagination mixed together to make him think he saw something he feared as a kid."

Mason finished wiping down the last of the dining room tables, then walked to the front counter where Eaver was cleaning. "So what do you think he actually saw that night?"

"Hell, I have no idea. It might've been a gator that he spooked, or a big ol' cat' swimming up close to shore, or it could've been something as little as bullfrogs or turtles getting in the water. Who knows? Depends on what he was drinking, too."

Mason laughed a little. "That's true. Does he still make his own moonshine?"

Eaver nodded. "You know he does. Got the same little still set up behind his house. Now come on back here and we'll get started on the kitchen. Then we'll just sweep the floors and get on outta here."

Mason rounded the corner of the counter and joined Eaver by the cash register. While she was placing a fresh trash bag in the receptacle, his eyes scanned the pass-through to the kitchen. He spotted Cinch's shiny cleaver, stuck in a slab of butcher block, and he pulled it out to admire it up close.

Eaver saw her friend holding the large cleaver. "Careful, Mason, Cinch keeps that thing razor sharp."

It looked it. Rather than satisfying his curiosity, Mason decided to set it gently on the counter. "Yeah, probably not for the average Joe to mess with. Well, if anyone is a master of cutlery and cookware, it's ol' Cinch."

He took up a rag and started helping Eaver clean the blue and white ceramic tiles covering the walls behind the counter.

The entryway door opened, sounding the little bell above it.

"Sorry, we're closed," Eaver called out. She craned her neck around the corner to see who had come in. Three figures had entered the restaurant, and were closing and locking the door. Then they turned to face her.

It was Malcolm Gibbs and his crew.

Oh shit, thought Mason when he saw their faces, *what are they doing here?*

"We ain't here to eat," said Big Mal. He and his cohorts approached the counter, staring at the pair on the other side. Mal looked angry; his large frame, two inches taller than Mason's, was tensed and his square jaw was set in a scowl. He directed his eyes to Mason.

"We been lookin' for you, Red." He walked to the opening at the end of the counter.

Mason felt his adrenaline pumping, just like when he used to encounter Big Mal in high school. He tried to stay calm. "Oh? Why's that, Mal?"

"Don't play stupid with me," warned Mal, stepping around the counter. "We know it was you who destroyed my greenhouse."

Mason, shocked by this serious accusation, shrank back a bit closer to Eaver. "What are you talking about? I wouldn't even know where it was!"

Big Mal was now behind the counter, nothing separating him from his mark. "You're the fancy ol' college boy, with access to things like sulfur. Which is what my whole greenhouse smelled like!"

"Mal, listen. First of all, going to college doesn't mean bringing chemicals back home with me. Secondly, why on Earth would I want to ruin your greenhouse? It would serve me no purpose, now would it?"

"Don't talk down to me, you little inbred runt!"

Runt? thought Mason. *I'm over six feet tall! This guy is clearly a mental marvel.* "I'm just saying," Mason reasoned, "that I've got no reason to do anything like that. You've got the wrong guy."

"Besides," Eaver added, "the same thing happened to our smokehouse out back. Same nasty smell was in there, too."

"Sure," scoffed Jesse. "You probably did it to make it look like the same thing happened to you. So we wouldn't suspect you."

"That's just plain crazy," said Mason. "Listen to yourselves."

Mal smirked. "I know you had something to do with it. You've always had a beef with us, ever since junior high."

"I wouldn't say *that*, exactly, but you *did* always bully me –"

"And your little bitch friend Eaver-Beaver probably told you where my shit was." He glanced in Eaver's direction. "Maybe I oughta do to this place what y'all did to mine."

"Don't you dare do anything to this restaurant," Eaver cautioned. "I'll have you locked up faster than you can say 'I'm a dipshit'."

"*Fuck* you! I'll do whatever the fuck I want, to whoever's got it comin'!" Mal's voice was growing in volume and intensity. He was clearly ready to erupt violently. "And I'll put anyone who fucks with me in the hospital!" He continued his advance.

Mason looked around nervously, trying to find a way out of their predicament. His eyes spotted the cleaver on the counter. He picked it up.

"Now just hold it, Mal," said Mason, trying to be assertive. "You can't come in here and threaten us. There are witnesses in this room. This is private property, and you need to leave."

"Whatcha gonna do, killer?" Mal scoffed. "Chop me up? You a secret *killer*, Red? You better not have had anything to do with what happened to Walt, you little inbred runt!"

"Easy, Mal, just back off." Mason had retreated as far as he could; he and Eaver were cornered against the tiled walls. His pulse was racing.

Big Mal snarled, reared back his right arm, and threw a strong punch at Mason. Panicking, Mason raised the cleaver in front of him. Mal's fist struck the sharp blade, ramming the cleaver against Mason's shoulder. Flesh and muscle instantly gave way to the steel, and Mal's hand split halfway to the wrist.

Mason, at the sight of what just happened, involuntarily opened his hands and let go of the cleaver. It slid loose from Mal's hand and fell to the floor with a heavy clang.

Mal screamed – not from pain, but rather from shock – and stared incredulously at what used to be his powerful hand. Then the blood began to pour out.

"*Holyfuck! Holyfuck!*" exclaimed Jesse, his face white. "We gotta do something! He's bleedin' like a stuck pig!"

Mitch ran behind the counter, his eyes darting for something to stop the bleeding. He spotted a dishrag, wrapped it tightly around Mal's hand, and grabbed his leader by the arm. "C'mon, dude, we gotta get you out of here. You need to go to the hospital."

Speechless, but mouth still agape, Mal clenched his wounded hand and let Mitch guide him around the counter, through the restaurant, and outside. Then the three drug dealers sped away, driving directly to Sweetboro Medical Center.

Mason, numb with shock, slowly turned around to face Eaver. Her hands remained pressed to her face, just below her wide, shaken eyes. After a minute, the words were finally able to leave his lips.

"Holy shit…"

CHAPTER 17

Eaver called her mother immediately to let her know what had happened. Sherrie instructed her to wait for her there and touch nothing, saying she was going to call the sheriff and have him meet everybody there at the restaurant. By the time the sheriff and his deputy got there to sort it out and take statements, Sherrie was waiting outside to bring them in.

Mason and Eaver sat anxiously at one of the dining tables. They were visibly shaken; Mason was squirming and rubbing his left shoulder, and Eaver's hands were trembling slightly. Neither of them could shed the image of Mal's hand splitting apart. They stood when they saw Sheriff Steele and Deputy Riggins enter the restaurant.

"Howdy Miss Eaver, Mason," said the sheriff. "Sit on down."

They did, and he and Carl took seats across from them. Sheriff Steele removed his hat and set it on the corner of the table. Sherrie stood next to the table, glancing at the blood trail on the floor.

"So what happened tonight?" Steele asked. "I understand you injured Malcolm Gibbs here?"

"We closed the restaurant and started cleaning up," said Eaver. "Then Mal and his pals, Mitch and Jesse, come in, bringing trouble."

"They were angry," Mason added. "Said crazy stuff like we had destroyed their greenhouse and left it stinking like sulfur. Which of course we didn't do. I wouldn't even know where to find his greenhouse."

"So he thought you destroyed his property, and came here to retaliate?"

Eaver nodded. "He was pissed. Even threatened to trash the restaurant, but I warned him not to. Then he came up on Mason here and tried to punch him."

"He had us cornered behind the counter there," said Mason, pointing to the tight spot where it happened. "I was holding

Cinch's cleaver in front of me, he took a swing, and all I could do was raise it up. He punched the cleaver, which – um – sliced his hand open."

Carl winced. "Oh lordy."

"It was self-defense, Sheriff," Mason insisted. "An involuntary defense mechanism, resulting in Mal unintentionally injuring himself. I swear I didn't *attack* him with a meat cleaver."

"Is that right?" the sheriff asked Eaver.

"Yessir. That's exactly what happened. Then, when the blood started gushing, Mitch and Jesse wrapped a towel around his hand and took him to the hospital."

"Jesus," said Sherrie, shaking her head.

The sheriff got up from the table, followed by the deputy, and walked around the counter. He saw a sizeable amount of blood on the tile floor, right where Mason had said. But not much anywhere else. If Mason had attacked Mal, Mal would've run from there while openly bleeding. But there was nothing more than droplets leading from there to the front door. So Mal must have stayed in that spot until his friends wrapped his hand to quell the bleeding. What the sheriff saw on the floor confirmed the story he had been told. Plus, he would never picture level-headed Mason as the type to go crazy and attack somebody. The sheriff looked at his deputy. "Okay," he said. "Looks about right."

Then he glanced out to the dining area. "In all my years I've never heard of something like this. I guess there's always a first time. We'll call you down to the station if we need you, but I don't think we'll need to. This is pretty cut and dry."

"No pun intended," said Deputy Riggins, who received a scowl from his boss.

The sheriff walked back to the table. "You know I have to go track down Mitch and Jesse, get their statements as well."

"Of course," said Mason. "Can't imagine they'll say anything contrary to what we told you. Even *they* would have to admit I didn't attack Mal. They're probably still over at the hospital."

Sheriff Steele returned his hat to his head, adjusted it, and said, "Alright, now, y'all try to have a good rest of your evening. We're all done here. C'mon, Spud." The policemen exited the restaurant and hustled through the rain to their town cruiser.

When the police had driven away, Sherrie turned to her

daughter. "Are you okay?"

Eaver nodded. "Yeah, I feel better now, after getting the police stuff out of the way." She glanced at the trickles of blood on the floor. "I guess now we can clean up the crime scene."

She pushed her chair back and stood. When Mason pushed against the table to do the same, he grunted in pain.

"What's the matter?" Eaver asked.

"My shoulder really hurts," said Mason, "where the cleaver struck me."

She walked to him and pulled his collar out to get a look inside. "That's bruising up pretty good. He must've put a lot of force into that punch."

"Enough to tear his hand wide open," Mason pointed out.

"I never saw so much blood," said Eaver.

Mason grinned. "Makes you think twice about wanting your crab cakes and ketchup, doesn't it?"

She didn't skip a beat. "Never. I'd eat some right now if we had some made. I'd have one in my mouth while cleaning up the blood."

Sherrie just shook her head. "You ain't right, daughter."

Mason got up and started walking toward the kitchen. "You got a mop?" he asked.

"Yeah," said Eaver. "I'll take care of that, how about you finish the counters?"

"Deal."

Eaver found the mop and bucket in the bathroom, filled the bucket with soap and water, then brought it behind the counter. She looked at Mason. "I still can't believe he called you 'killer'."

"Don't forget 'little inbred runt'."

Eaver remembered and started giggling. "Oh yeah, bless his dumb ol' heart."

"You two aren't very nice," said Sherrie.

"Why?" her daughter asked. "Just because Killer here tried to chop Mal's hand off?"

The comment caught Mason by surprise and he burst out laughing.

"That's not funny," Sherrie tried to state, but a smile was breaking on her lips. Then, seeing Mason's face turning red from laughing, she said, "Okay, it's a little funny."

The rumble of thunder was heard, louder than before. The rainstorm was getting stronger. Sherrie took notice, looking at the ceiling. She stood up to help her daughter, and a yawn forced its way through her mouth.

Eaver took pity on her mother; it had been a stressful day for the restaurant owner. "Go on home, Momma, we can take care of this."

"Are you sure? I don't mind."

"No, scram. This won't take us very long."

Sherrie appreciated it. "Okay, sweetie, thanks. Hurry home. And Mason, thank you for helping out today. You're such a sweetheart."

"Don't mention it," he smiled. "Happy to help."

Sherrie leaned over the counter, kissed Eaver's cheek, and left to go home.

The rainfall intensified while Mason and Eaver worked. By the time Mason had wiped everything down and Eaver had cleaned all the blood from the floor, the rain was pelting the roof pretty good.

"Listen to that," Eaver remarked while stowing the mop in the bathroom. "Maybe we should wait it out a little until it dies down."

"Fine with me," said Mason, who had no particular desire to be drenched. The rain would lighten up again before long, and then they could lock up the restaurant and leave.

Suddenly they heard a loud *WHAP*, accompanied by the sound of glass cracking. They looked in the direction of the startling sound and saw pieces of a broken window fall to the floor and shatter. A mysterious shape was visible just outside the window frame. Mason's first thought was that Mitch or Jesse had come back for vengeance. But then the shape pulled itself inside the restaurant, and Mason saw something much more frightening than Mal's cronies.

This thing wasn't even human.

A dark, bulky mass dropped to the floor, collected itself, and stood to face its quarry. A menacing hiss burst from its mouth. Eaver screamed, and her knees buckled involuntarily.

Mason could not believe his eyes. He seemed to be staring at some kind of sea monster. The thing was about five feet tall, with slick, shiny, dark green skin, a thick tail, stout legs with webbed feet, and six appendages – three on each side – that looked like tentacles, each with a long, white claw at the tip.

But the head was the most terrifying. It was the size of a man's, but with a protruding snout – the lower jaw extending farther than the upper – full of needle-like teeth. The only feature more horrific than the creature's mouth was the pair of bulbous black eyes bulging from their sockets.

Hissing again, it lashed out with one of its appendages. The four-foot tentacle struck the edge of one of the wooden tables with sizable force, busting the board it hit.

"Stay back!" said Mason. "That thing's strong!" He positioned himself between the monster and Eaver.

"Jesusgodjesus," she muttered, quivering from shock.

Another swing of its tentacle missed Mason and whacked a wall, knocking down two oars hung in the shape of an X. They landed on a table, one of them bouncing in Mason's direction. He quickly reached down for it, and gripped it desperately with his shaking hands.

Mason waved the oar aggressively in front of him, hoping to scare the creature away. The action seemed to entice it further, and it advanced rapidly. Mason took a swing at the thing's head. The creature swiped at the oar, deflecting it against a table. The force broke the oar, which split just above the paddle.

The stem of the oar remained in Mason's hands. Looking at the end, he noticed it had not broken cleanly. A sharp, jagged point was left at the far end. *A spear, then,* he granted.

Fighting his racing heartbeat, he focused on engaging the monster that was coming for him. He jabbed at the thing, but a tentacle repelled the oar. Trying to time his attack against the motion of the appendages, he plunged the oar handle forward once more.

This time he stabbed the creature. The broken tip punched through the flesh and deep into the body.

The thing went crazy. Appendages flailing wildly, it erupted with a coarse, raspy squeal. It recoiled, pulling itself away. Mason held firm to the oar, and it slipped out of its victim. A good-sized hole was left in the creature's midsection, blackish blood oozing from the wound and spilling onto the floor. In pain, the monster retreated and disappeared out the window.

Then it was gone.

Pale with shock, Mason turned his head to check on Eaver. She drew her eyes away from the window to meet his gaze. She looked at the dazed young man holding the bloodied oar handle.

"Not bad for a little inbred runt," she said.

CHAPTER 18

"So let me get this straight," Sheriff Steele murmured, rubbing his temples. "You called me out here again to report that you've been attacked by a *sea monster?*"

Sherrie folded her arms, also eyeing the young adults with skepticism. "My sentiments exactly."

"I know it sounds bonkers," said Mason. "But that's what happened! I wouldn't have believed it myself if I hadn't seen it. It was the scariest thing I've ever seen." The image of the horrific creature was burned into his brain, and probably would be forever.

"It was like something out of a nightmare," Eaver added. "Like I said, it had tentacles, legs, a big tail, huge, scary eyes, and sharp teeth."

Mason pointed to the table with the broken board. "And lots of strength."

The sheriff could not deny that damage had been done to the restaurant since he was there earlier. Pieces of glass were scattered across the floor near the broken window, drywall was dented and smudged where things had been knocked off, and the wooden table Mason was referring to had one of its planks busted in half. "This place has taken a little beating, that much is apparent."

Sherrie buried her face in her hands. "This has not been a good day for my restaurant."

Eaver reached over and hugged her mother. "I'm sorry, Momma. We'll get it fixed up, don't worry."

Sherrie rolled her eyes. "I know, I know, but it still sucks. Between the smokehouse, the meat lost, the injury to Malcolm, and now the window."

"Even so," said Mason, "we'll all help out and get things back to normal."

"Although nothing about this is normal at the moment," Eaver pointed out.

"One thing's for damn sure," stated Sherrie. "I'm bringing the shotgun here from home. I could use the protection, whether it's against violent thugs or friggin' sea monsters."

"Wouldn't be a bad idea," admitted the sheriff. Then he added, "For any intruder, even if it's just to scare them away. Although I don't think you have to worry about sea monsters."

Eaver's back stiffened. "You don't think we're *lying*, do you?"

"I don't know *what* to think. I don't think you'd lie to me, but at the same time listen to what you're saying. How do you expect me to take something like that?"

"I feel you, Sheriff," said Mason. "And we'd think the same if the roles were reversed. But look at the blood it left! And smell that nasty odor it brought with it!"

Sheriff Steele nodded. "I noticed that, like rotten eggs. You say that's what the creature smelled like?"

"Yep. As soon as it broke in we could smell it."

"That's the same stink that was all over the busted smokehouse this morning," Eaver said. "I think now we know what destroyed the smokehouse."

"And," added Mason, "Mal said something about his greenhouse stinking like sulfur. These things must've been responsible for that too."

"Jesus," said Eaver, staring blindly at the floor. "How many of them do you think are out there?"

Mason shrugged. "I'm still trying to wrap my head around the one."

Sheriff Steele walked toward the pools of black liquid on the floor. "This where you say you stabbed it?"

"Yes sir, then it went back through the window."

"It does look like some kind of blood," the sheriff acknowledged, "but not like what I'm used to seeing." He knelt down to get a closer look. "It's almost black, and gooey." The sulfuric stench was much stronger near the blood. "Damn, that's a strong stink."

The others joined him, hovering over the liquid. "I don't know of any animal whose blood smells like sulfur," Mason remarked.

"Well, let's not touch it," said Steele. "Sherrie, do you have something I can use to take a sample of this to my lab analyst?"

"Yeah," she nodded. "I'll go get you something." She went to the kitchen, dug around for a moment, and returned with a Tupperware container and steel spatula. "Will this work?"

"Perfect, thank you." The sheriff then scooped some of the viscous fluid off the floor and dumped it into the plastic container. Then he pressed the lid on tightly and stood up. "I'll get this to Marty, see what he can make of it."

"Marty Bennett, the diver?" asked Sherrie.

"Yes ma'am. He's my diver, scientist, analyst, you name it. He's my go-to guy."

Sheriff Steele followed the dark droplets that led from the pooled mess to the window. Upon inspection of the window frame, he spotted moist, slimy residue on the frame and remaining shards of glass. The sulfuric stench was there as well. *What could this stuff have come from?* he pondered, baffled. Maybe the kids were telling the truth about some strange sea creature.

"Speaking of Marty," the sheriff said, recalling what the diver had reported to him, "he told me about some unusual findings in Pirate's Bend. He was diving there, looking for Earl Goates, and found an underwater cavern. Thinks it was underneath Pirate's Point. He said there were some animals inside, but he couldn't see what they were. He got spooked and high-tailed it out of there. But maybe they were what you saw tonight."

Sherrie had heard about the old fisherman's disappearance. "So no luck finding Earl yet?" she enquired.

"Afraid not. And his boat was banged up. At this point, unfortunately, we have to assume that his body won't be recovered."

"He could've been killed by one of those things!" said Eaver.

"Or," the sheriff offered, "he simply could've been drinking, hit the rocks, and drowned. Then the ocean could've taken his body away. There's no way of knowing."

"No matter what happened to him," Mason declared, "one thing is undeniable."

"What's that, son?"

"We've got monsters, Sheriff."

CHAPTER 19

Tammy Todd was stressed out. In addition to her fighting with the bank and trying to keep her house, she had recently discovered suspicious text messages on her boyfriend's phone. And now she was fretful because Joe hadn't bothered to see her at all today and he was not answering his phone. She feared he had become bored with her and was out sleeping with somebody else. The last place Tammy wanted to be right now was at work. She thought about calling in sick, but she was more responsible than that. She was the only nurse tonight at Sweetboro Medical Center.

It wasn't that hectic of a night there anyway. The most notable patients were the needy new mother, the crazy guy rambling about monsters, and the young man who somehow split his hand to the meaty part of his palm. Other than that it was pretty dull. It would be an easy shift.

Tammy made her hourly rounds, checking on her few patients. She changed IVs and passed meds as required. Careful not to wake those who were asleep, she finished her rounds and walked the quiet hallway to the front desk.

The chubby security guard, Murph, was stationed there alone, as he was every night. He turned his head when he heard Tammy appear through the door. "How's it going, Tam?" he asked with a genial smile.

Tammy sighed. "Not so good, Murph."

The guard frowned. "Why? What's the matter?"

She leaned on the reception desk. "I don't know what to do about Joe."

"You two having trouble?"

"Yeah. I went through his phone last night, and saw he's been texting someone I didn't know. Let's just say the conversation seemed inappropriate."

Murph sat up a little straighter. "Oh no. I'm sorry, hon. Did you ask him about it?"

She shook her head, making the curls of her short, black hair waggle. "No, he didn't even bother to come see me today. And I can't get hold of him on his phone. I swear, he's out with someone else and I'm gonna lose him." Her voice began to quiver. "I just don't know what to do."

Murph stood up and rested a hand on her shoulder. "Hey now, you're gonna be fine. If he's the type to jump from woman to woman, then you don't want him in your life anyway. Right?"

Tammy nodded. "Right."

"So hell with him, if that's what he's all about. You deserve better."

"I know, I know, you're right. It just sucks losing someone, you know?"

"I do indeed. Been down that road a few times myself. But the Lord never puts anything in our paths that we can't handle. Everything will work out the way it's supposed to. Just be patient and keep moving forward."

Tammy brought her hand up to his and patted it gently. "Thank you, Murph. I needed to hear that right now. You're the best."

"My pleasure, Tam. Now go relax." He held up the book he was reading and grinned. "That's what I'll be doing."

"Alright, Murph. I'll come bug you a little later." Then Tammy retreated through the hallway door and returned to her station.

She sat for a few minutes, reflecting on what old Murph said. His points were valid, but that didn't make it hurt any less. Before long, Tammy was feeling stressed again.

She needed a cigarette. Or two.

Her rounds were recently finished, so there was no reason why she shouldn't go take a smoke break. It was still raining outside, but she could go outside through the receiving door and stay dry under the metal awning there.

Tammy made sure she had her cigarettes and lighter, then strolled toward the receiving area. On the way, she decided to take one more quick look at one of the patients before going outside.

She quietly opened the door to Malcolm Gibbs's room. Keeping the light off, she made her way to his IV, which was only slightly lower than it was the last time she checked. Pausing to look at his bandaged hand, she wondered what it would be like to have her hand cleaved in half. She shivered. Then she left, closing the door to keep it dark for the sleeping patient.

Tammy got to the receiving area, swung the door open to the outside alley, and pushed the cinder block in place with her foot to prop it open. Next she pulled a cigarette from her pack and lit it, drawing the smoke deeply.

The satisfying smoke, combined with the sound of the rain around her, began to ease her. After a while, she realized Murph was right. She would get through this, as well as every other obstacle in her life. She took another drag and focused on the soothing harmony of the rain and the nearby ocean waves.

A rustling in the bushes caught her attention.

Tammy drew her eyes straight ahead to where the sound was coming from, and focused intently. She was leery about critters, and had been since her childhood. Whether it was a possum, armadillo, or raccoon, she had always been a little afraid of them.

Something moved again, this time fifteen feet to her left. Her head followed the rustling sound, and now she noticed an unpleasant smell in the rainy air. It smelled a bit like sewage, and she wondered for a second if a sewer drain had backed up nearby.

Suddenly something burst forth from where she had heard the first rustling. By the time she brought her eyes back to the spot, a dark shape was rushing toward her. She did not have any time to react before she was struck by something that yanked her legs out from under her. She landed hard on the cement and was instantly pulled out into the rain.

With a scream, Tammy kicked and squirmed against the painful pressure as she was dragged violently across the alley and into the bushes.

As her flailing hands disappeared into the brush, two other creatures emerged from the shadows. They slowly approached the open door and, curious, proceeded inside the hospital.

CHAPTER 20

Malcolm Gibbs woke up in pain. The morphine had already worn off, and his hand felt like it was throbbing. Mal found the morphine pump with his good hand and pressed the button to receive another dose. As the medication kicked in, he gazed down at his bandaged hand and sighed.

The doctor had stitched Mal's hand back together and bandaged it after surgery. Mal would recover, although it would take a lot of time and rehab before he would have full use of his hand again. The surgery was successful, but Mal had lost a lot of blood. So he would be spending the night in this small hospital bed, married to an IV bag for fluid replacement.

He had no idea what time it was. It didn't really matter; it was the middle of the night and the hospital was dark and quiet. He appreciated the quiet more than anything. The asshole in the next room had been driving Mal crazy earlier with his frantic ravings. Now he had finally stopped. Maybe the doctor sedated him, maybe he went to sleep, maybe he died. Mal didn't care, as long as he had eventually shut up.

Mal's mouth was dry and sticky. Having to reach across his body with his left hand, he grabbed the plastic cup of water on his tray table. The water was room temperature, but that was just fine. Anything to moisten his mouth and throat.

Drinking slowly, he pondered the crazy man in the next room. He was being brought in at the same time Mal came out of surgery. Mal remembered scoffing silently hearing about the man's minor injury. The pussy was ranting wildly about being scratched by a terrible monster. Mal was sure the man would prefer scratches to having his hand split in half.

The man was hysterical for what seemed like hours, driving Mal nuts. He went on and on about some unbelievable monster by the river – he was clearly on some kind of hallucinogen – and was imagining that the scratching had somehow poisoned him and was burning him up. Mal didn't believe a bit of it, although he did overhear the doctor saying something about worsening fever and sweating. Mal shrugged it off as symptoms of whatever drugs the man had obviously overdosed on.

That guy just needs to buy some of my weed, thought Mal. He chuckled quietly. Then he remembered what had happened to his greenhouse, and his grin dissolved into a scowl. It was going to take some work to repair the greenhouse, which he could no longer do with his damaged hand. His buddies could do the work, he figured, but he was sure they wouldn't do anything until Mal was there to direct them. And the longer he was stuck in the hospital, the more vulnerable his plants were. Frustration overtook him.

He was certain Mason had something to do with the destruction of his greenhouse. That little twerp thought he was getting some payback for being picked on all those years. Maybe even thought it would impress his girlfriend Eaver. *Well*, Mal vowed silently, *that sumbitch is gonna get what's coming to him.* Mal was going to make Mason pay somehow, whether beating him to a pulp or burning his house down – anything to make an example out of him.

Nobody fucked with Big Mal without paying the price.

He just had to be smart about it. Getting caught by the police was not an acceptable risk, so obviously beating Mason up was out. If he was going to destroy Mason's property instead, he would have to leave no evidence. And have an alibi. That wouldn't be too difficult.

The rainstorm was worsening again. The pelting of the window glass grew louder. Then Mal saw a bright flash followed by the roar of thunder. *Lovely weather*, Mal noted, shaking his head. At least his plants were getting watered. That thought reminded him of his own thirst, and he grabbed the cup to take another drink of the tepid water.

He heard what sounded like something breaking in the next room. Tilting his head, he listened for more. Another flash of lightning burst outside, and thunder immediately followed. *Shut up*, Mal cursed to the storm, *I'm trying to hear what's going on in here.*

When the rumble subsided, Mal could again listen for sounds in the next room. He focused on the wall separating the rooms and listened intently. *What broke in there?* he mused. It could have been a nurse checking on the patient and accidentally dropping something. Or it could have been the patient trying to get up and move around unsuccessfully.

Great, he thought. *Now that crazy asshole is awake again and will keep raving about monsters.* But after three minutes of anticipation, he was relieved to hear nothing else from the adjacent room.

There was a thud at his door, and it startled him. Mal tried to sit up, looking through the dark toward the door to his room. Another thud, some fumbling with the handle, and then the door opened.

Mal watched as a broad silhouette entered the room. The door closed behind it, casting the room in darkness once more. And he smelled the same rotten egg odor he recalled from his greenhouse.

"Nurse?" he called out, but got no reply. "What's going on?"

All he heard was a sound on the floor, like someone mopping it. *What the fuck?* he thought. *Who the hell's in here?* Then he heard wet, smacking sounds, getting closer and closer to his bed. And the horrible stink was growing stronger. It was definitely not the nurse who had entered his room.

Something horrible – something hellish – was with him instead.

Mal quickly reached for his cell phone, his hand fumbling around the tray table until he found it. He pressed the button on the side of his phone, instantly activating the screen light.

He saw a ghastly face in the dim light, inches above his own.

Mal convulsed and screamed. He attempted to get up from the bed, but suddenly a heavy limb fell across his chest to hold him down. He lashed out at the creature, striking cold, slimy, yet firm skin. Then something restrained his arms. He struggled but was powerless to move. The phone now lay face-up on his chest, and the screen light illuminated the nightmare before him.

Some kind of animal, monster, devil had him. It had bulbous eyes, slick, fishy skin, and a wide snout with long teeth. Mal's eyes were frozen on those of the monster. They were the size of billiard balls, black orbs covered by a milky lens when the creature blinked.

Mal continued to lock unbelieving eyes with the thing while

he endured what felt like talons penetrating deep and tearing open tissue. He could feel the warmth of his own blood flow out over his body. The creature hissed, sticky strands of saliva stretching as its jaws opened, and Mal breathed the odor from its mouth.

The last thing Malcolm Gibbs saw was a mouthful of needle-like teeth closing in around his face.

CHAPTER 21

The book was getting really good. Murph had enjoyed the works of James Patterson for over a decade, and this latest novel did not disappoint. Murph was a lucky man; he had a quiet, easy job that allowed him to relax, eat snacks, and read books with very infrequent interruption. It was ideal.

If he were married, his wife would tell him he needed a better job that would give him more exercise. His doctor would agree, especially since his weight and blood pressure had increased every year. But this lazy night job made him content.

Out of the corner of his eye, he thought he saw movement on the video monitor. He turned his head to check, but saw nothing on the black and white screen but the peaceful hallway. After a few seconds to confirm all was well, he returned his attention to his rousing book.

Then another movement on the screen caught his eye again.

Murph glanced at the monitor, and this time he saw a figure moving. Just for a split second, though, before it vanished into one of the patients' rooms.

That wasn't Tammy, he noted. He didn't see much, but he knew what he saw was not the white uniform of his favorite nurse. The shape was dark, and heftier.

The portly security guard raised an eyebrow in concern. There were no visitors this time of night, and no staff on duty that looked like that. He had better go investigate.

Laboring to his feet, Murph made his way around the reception desk and through the door to the main hall. *Probably one of the patients wandering around*, he figured. But he had to make sure that was the case, and if it was, that the patient was okay.

He had almost reached the end of the corridor when the odor invaded his nose. *What the hell?* he winced, smelling the rotten-egg stench of sulfur. It made him stop and look around, confused as to what could cause that smell. There were two rooms ahead of him before the hallway ended; perhaps the stench was coming from one of the patients' rooms.

Murph continued down the hall and to the door to Mal's room. He reached for the handle and started to push the door open, reminding himself to stay quiet in case there was a sleeping patient inside.

Then he heard a sharp noise, like a steel tray hitting the floor, down the adjacent hallway around the corner. Jumping, his eyes darted toward the mouth of that corridor. Whatever it was sounded like it was about twenty or thirty feet away from his position.

The security guard hurried around the corner and down the left hallway. "Tammy?" he called out. "Is that you?"

No answer was heard in the quiet hallway. The only sounds were those of Murph's brisk footsteps against the tile. The nasty odor was still heavy in the air, and Murph furrowed his brow in concern; hopefully it was not some kind of gas leak. He quickened his pace.

Then, when he rounded another corner, he caught a glimpse of a patient's door closing. He slowed down as he approached the door. Taking a deep breath to calm his labored heartbeat, he reached for the door handle, turned it, and silently pushed the door open.

The room was dark, except for the bit of light coming in from the hallway. Murph saw a shiny shape at the side of the bed. An eerie feeling washed over him as he realized something was not right. He flipped the light switch on the wall.

The light revealed what looked like some kind of amphibious creature in the room. Wet, olive-green skin covered a horrific form. The nightmarish thing was hovering over a female patient in the bed. It looked like it was *eating* the woman.

Murph was in shock and had no idea what to do. He just knew he needed to do something. The security guard instinctively pulled his nightstick and stepped closer.

Just then he heard movement behind the door. He whirled in time to catch sight of a second creature. As the monster spread its appendages and attacked, Murph suddenly went into cardiac arrest.

He felt severe pain in his chest, and lost his ability to breathe, move, or think. Everything instantly went black as he fell helpless to the ground. Murph was dead before the talons began to cut into him.

CHAPTER 22

Sheriff Steele was awakened by the annoying ringing of his phone. Shaking himself back to consciousness, he rolled over on the bed and groped for the cell phone. He answered it while focusing his fuzzy eyes on the clock to see that it was just after six.

Lewis Simkins, the officer on duty at the station, was on the other end. With panic in his voice, he informed his boss that some people had been murdered at the hospital. Steele rose from the bed and took the phone to the hallway, hoping to let his wife get back to sleep. There he conversed further, gathering all the information his deputy had about this shocking incident. Then he stated he would get to the hospital right away and hung up.

He closed his eyes and shook his head, still in disbelief over what he was just told. This was a small, peaceful town – until the events of the last few days. Now there were missing people, a violent confrontation that put somebody in the hospital, astonishing claims of monsters, and now some deaths at Sweetboro Medical Center. The sheriff was in for another long day.

After throwing on his uniform and kissing his wife, he started his cruiser and headed straight to the hospital. He yawned deeply as he drove. Between how crazy yesterday was, with Malcolm Gibbs and then the alleged monster attack, how late it was when he finally got home and went to bed, and how early in the morning the phone woke him up, he was exhausted. He was definitely going to need a good night's sleep tonight.

He arrived at the hospital around 6:30. The chief physician was waiting for him outside the main entrance. It was Dr. John Warden, who also happened to be the town coroner, and he looked extremely relieved to see the sheriff.

"Thank God you're here," the doctor exhaled. "It's terrible inside."

"What happened, Doc?"

"At shift change this morning, one of the orderlies starting her shift – Becky Salinger – discovered the bodies."

"How many?"

"Two for sure," said the doctor, glancing at the charts in his hands. "Malcolm Gibbs, and Billy Castle. And maybe three more."

The sheriff shifted uncomfortably. "What do you mean?"

"Shirley Franklin gave birth here yesterday, but her body is missing now. And so is our night nurse Tammy Todd. And Murph, the security guard, is gone too."

"So possibly as many as five dead. C'mon, Doc, let's get in there and figure it out."

Dr. Warden led the sheriff inside, past the traumatized staff huddled in the waiting room, and through the door to the main hall. The sheriff's heartbeat increased with each step, as he tried to imagine what the crime scenes would look like.

"Did they steal any drugs?" he asked while following the chief physician.

"No, the dispensary was untouched. Besides, whatever killed these people was not after drugs – it couldn't even be human."

"What?" said Steele, feeling nervous; this was starting to remind him of last night's claims of sea monsters at the restaurant.

"Come on, I'll show you."

Dr. Warden led the sheriff down the hallway to the nearest room of incident. As they neared, Sheriff Steele could smell the same sulfuric odor that was in the damaged restaurant. And he could see a dirty trail that had dried on the tile floor. He had a bad feeling about this.

"This is where Mrs. Franklin was," said the doctor, opening the door with his gloved hand. Then he stood aside so the sheriff could enter.

The room was in disarray. Metal trays and blankets were strewn on the floor, and the bed was overturned on its side. The sheriff immediately noticed the blood on the mattress. Stepping closer, he saw spatter patterns that would indicate somebody was cut into forcibly while on the bed. The blood trail then continued across the room to the window, which had been broken outward.

A new mom, he noted, shaking his head. He turned toward the doctor. "And the baby? Was it in here too?"

"No, she's in NICU so we can monitor her; she had the umbilical wrapped around her throat during birth. But she looks like she'll be fine."

"Thank God." The sheriff looked at the bloody drag trail again. "Well, based on the amount of blood lost here, I'd wager Mrs. Franklin isn't alive. Somebody attacked her in bed, dragged her to the window, and busted it out and left with her. But why take the body?"

"Um, I have a theory, but you need to see the other victims first."

The sheriff looked quizzically at the chief physician, then figured the man knew what he was talking about. "Okay," Steele said guardedly. "Let's see the others now."

They moved to the room where the first body was found. The corpse lay serenely on the bed, but there was nothing serene about its appearance. The patient had gaping holes in his neck, torso, and legs, and his entire body was covered in dried blood.

"Look closer," said the doctor. "These are bites. Note the tearing and stretching of the tissue – not caused by any cutting instrument. It looks more like what you'd see from the bite of a small sand tiger shark."

The sheriff was stunned. "What the hell kind of man would take bites out of another human being?"

"No man, I'm afraid. It has to be a large animal of some sort. The bite radius would indicate a larger mouth than any man, plus the points of initial tissue breaching are pointed, jagged – not caused by the straight, lineal bite from a man's teeth."

"Jesus. Same with the other victim?"

"Yes. Come on, he's just next door."

They walked to the adjacent room, and the sheriff was treated to another grisly scene. The body on the bed was twisted, indicating a struggle before dying. Like the other patient, this bloodied corpse had large bites taken out of it. The victim's face was gone entirely. Just strands of muscle and exposed skull remained. Fighting the urge to vomit, Sheriff Steele looked away from the face and saw the bandaged hand.

"This must be Malcolm Gibbs," he reasoned, and the doctor nodded. "Unbelievable."

"So, now you can understand my theory, which is that something was here to *eat* people. Since the two victims here are partially eaten, it's a safe bet that's why they took Mrs. Franklin's body when they left."

"Shit, Doc," said the sheriff. "In all my years I've never seen anything close to this."

"Neither have I. And I'm a senior physician... as well as the damn coroner! Now you can see why I'm at such a loss right now. I can't imagine any type of animal that could've gotten inside the hospital and done this to them."

"Something strong enough to break the window in Mrs. Franklin's room and drag the body away," the sheriff added.

"You think that's how they got in?" asked Dr. Warden.

The sheriff shook his head. "No, the window was busted out from the inside. Plus, there's a dirty trail in the hallway that indicates something was moving through the hallway to get to the patients' rooms."

"How else could they get in?" the doctor posed. "Through the main entrance and past Murph?"

"No, the trail they left is just back here." The mention of the security guard made Sheriff Steele think of cameras. "You have security cameras, right?"

"Yeah, that's right! But only covering the halls, not in the rooms."

"That's alright," the sheriff assured. "I'm sure they had to be in the hallway at some point. Let's check your security cameras and see who or what did this."

Dr. Warden brought the sheriff back to the reception area and around the front desk. They sat, and the doctor pulled up last night's video surveillance footage from the security guard's computer there. Within minutes they had video images of the hallways.

"Okay, here we go," said the doctor. "Now we just have to scan back until we see something." He used the mouse to drag the timeline back slowly. Then he saw motion in the video, and he let it play in real time. What he and the sheriff saw on the screen was mindboggling.

Two bizarre figures quickly came into view, looking like something out of a science-fiction movie. They paused for a moment outside Billy Castle's room, and then pushed the door open and slipped inside.

"What the fuck was that?" Steele exclaimed. "Play that back!"

Speechless, the doctor backed the video up to watch again. The screen showed the creatures moving rapidly, stopping long enough for the camera to record their monstrous features. They looked something like a cross between an alligator, a squid, and a monster from another planet. The sheriff shuddered as he realized he was seeing exactly what Mason and Eaver had described to him last night.

After three minutes, one of the things came back into the hallway and went to Malcolm Gibbs's room. Two of its six tentacles tried to push the door open, then experimented with the handle until the door gave way. It vanished into Mal's room for several minutes. Then the video showed both creatures emerge from their rooms and swiftly disappear down another hallway toward Mrs. Franklin's room. Shortly after that they witnessed Murph coming into view, pausing at Mal's door, and then hurrying down the other hallway. Then nothing but a still corridor.

Dr. Warden backed it up one more time. When he saw a clear view of the monsters, he paused the image so he and the sheriff could study them.

"What in the name of God *are* they?"

"I – I have no idea, Sheriff. I'm still not sure if I'm having a crazy nightmare or not."

"Whatever they are, they're dangerous killers. We've established they're strong enough to break through windows, and we can see they are surprisingly quick."

"And poisonous, I'd wager," the doctor added.

"Huh?"

"Billy Castle, that first victim, was admitted last night. He was hysterical and claimed he had been scratched by a monster. Said he was burning and feeling very sick. He did have a fever, which rapidly worsened. I ordered hydration treatment and took some blood. Despite his bizarre claims, I thought he was just having a bad reaction to some kind of drug he had taken. But now, after all this, I'm afraid everything he said was true."

The sheriff stretched his arms behind his head. "So, let's see. We seem to have a monster problem in our town, something that lives in the water, they have deadly claws and teeth, and just for the icing on the cake they have some kind of poisonous venom." He sighed. "What a time for the mayor to be across the globe on a cruise."

"What are you going to do, Sheriff?"

Sheriff Steele stiffened his back. "I have a feeling I know where they live. In the meantime, no statements to the public until we figure out exactly what to say. But right now I'd like to take this footage back to the station for further study with the rest of my men."

"No problem," said Dr. Warden. "I'll copy it onto a flash drive for you." He reached into the top desk drawer and retrieved a portable USB drive. While the doctor was copying the files for him, the sheriff picked up his phone and called Marty.

"Hey Marty," Steele said when the diver answered, "it's Steele. Listen, there was an attack at the hospital and it was pretty bad. But we have video of the things that did it, and you have to see it to believe it. Nobody's ever seen anything like these things before."

"What, you mean animals?" Marty asked.

"More like sea monsters. This is right up your alley, and we're gonna need all your input. Meet me at the station, will ya? I'll be there shortly."

"Okay, Sheriff. On my way."

"Get ready to see something you'll never forget."

CHAPTER 23

By the time the sheriff squared things away at the hospital and returned to the station, Marty was already there. Seeing the sheriff pull up and park, Marty stepped out of his Dodge van and approached the cruiser.

"So?" he asked, oddly excited. "What've you got?"

Steele shook his head, still in shock over what he had seen. "Like I said, something you have to see to believe," he said. "I'm gonna need all your ideas on this one."

"You said sea monsters, were you being literal? Or was that just a figure of speech?"

"C'mon, Marty. You'll see for yourself." They walked to the front of the police station, and the sheriff opened the door.

Deputy Carl Riggins had just started his day and sent the old night officer home. He was at the front desk, having just hung up the phone he was speaking into. "Hey, boss," he said as the men walked inside. "Lena Dermont just called. She says her daughter Hannah is missing. Hasn't seen or heard from her in two days." Then, realizing the sheriff was dealing with more pressing matters, he asked "What's going on at the hospital?"

"We got us a situation, Spud," replied the sheriff. "At least two people were killed there last night. Probably four."

The deputy's eyes widened. "Holy Jesus. Lewis told me about the call when I got here, but I had no idea it was that bad."

"It gets worse. Come on back with us, I've got something crazy to show you. And then I'll need you to go notify next of kin."

Carl nodded. "Sure, boss. What exactly happened there?"

"Better if I just show you both," said Steele, leading the pair to his office. The group followed and waited earnestly while the sheriff woke his computer and inserted the flash drive into a USB port. After a moment, the files on the portable drive were displayed on the screen.

"Okay," the sheriff said, "here we go. Watch this." He double-clicked on the video file, and the footage began to run on the computer's default player.

The hallway footage from the hospital's security camera began to play. It took a few minutes for Steele to find the moment when the creatures appeared. When they did, Marty and Carl instinctively recoiled from the monitor.

"Jumpin' Jehoshaphat!" said the deputy. "What the hell is that?"

The sheriff pointed to the screen. "Watch, they go to the first victim's room, Billy Castle, one goes into Malcolm Gibbs's room, and then they head out to attack Mrs. Franklin. And watch how fast they can get around." He played back the entire sequence three times for the others, then paused the video to concentrate on an image of the creatures.

"What do you think?" the sheriff asked, turning to Marty.

"Wow... I don't know what to say. Okay, well, it's not from blue water, looks like something built to be on land. This would definitely live in the shallows, possibly in that cave I found."

"After seeing what it's capable of, I don't want you or anybody else diving in these waters," said Steele.

"Look at that thing," Marty marveled, his eyes glued to the screen. "I mean, Jesus... how does something like that exist without us knowing until now?"

"You got me," said Carl.

"Amazing... look how it's put together. It has clawed tentacles, probably to grab things from farther away than arms could, and legs to allow it to move on land like an amphibian. And obviously it can breathe in and out of the water, so it must have both gills and lungs, like some amphibians and fish. That tail looks like something from an alligator or dinosaur. The tail's weight probably helps stabilize it when it walks on land; and in the water it likely uses that tail to swim in an undulating motion."

"Jesus, Marty," winced the sheriff. "This isn't a goddamn biology lesson."

"It is for us," Marty replied. "The existence of this thing is *exactly* a biology lesson. We've never seen anything like this, ever.

Does this mean there are other surprises Mother Nature has yet to reveal to us? Something recently awakened by tectonic activity? Or is this thing some kind of result of mutation, due to environmental factors humans have caused?"

"Marty…"

"I know, I know, what to do about these things." The scientist cleared his throat. "Well, first thing I'd say we need to do is warn everybody about them."

Sheriff Steele shifted uncomfortably. "That's a slippery slope, Marty. I've thought of that, but then I just keep thinking about how the news would get onto the Internet. Then we'd get droves of yahoos coming in to look for monsters. That's a bunch more people that could get killed. I can't be responsible for that."

"Makes sense," said Marty. "But the townspeople do need to know. Word's gonna get around from the hospital employees."

"Of course we're notifying the families of the victims at the hospital. And we'll go door to door to at least let everybody know that people were killed by an animal attack and they should stay locked up at night until we find what did it. But other than that I want to keep a media lockdown on this. No mention of sea monsters."

"Secondly," continued Marty, "we need to find out where these things live and kill them. Normally I'm not for eradicating any species, but when they're a danger to the public, it's a different story. And the first place I'd look is that underwater cavern in Pirate's Bend."

"I think we should call in some help," Carl suggested. "We have no idea how many of these creatures there are, or how hard they'd be to kill. Maybe we should call the state boys?"

"Excellent idea, Spud. They could help us take care of this problem without it becoming a media circus." The sheriff pulled up the number for the state troopers on his computer. Then he activated the speakerphone on his desk phone and dialed the troopers.

After four rings they picked up. "State Patrol, this is Captain Moody."

Sheriff Steele had dealt with Josh Moody several times in the past, and he was glad to hear the familiar voice. "Hey, Captain, this is Sheriff Steele down in Sweetboro."

"Howdy, Jimmy. Long time no see. What can I do you for?"

The sheriff didn't know where to start. "Well, I'm not sure how to say this, so I'll just lay it on you, Josh. We had an attack at the hospital here in town last night, three to four people killed, and when I watched the surveillance video I saw the animals that did it."

There was a moment of silence before the trooper's voice was heard again from the phone speaker. "So some kind of animal broke into your hospital? Like a cougar?"

"Animals, yes, but nothing like you've ever seen before. These things are something nobody's seen before, something that lives in the ocean but can walk on land."

Another silent pause. "I don't think I follow, Jimmy."

The sheriff closed his eyes, knowing how ridiculous his next statement was going to sound. "They're some kind of killer sea monster. I'm asking for you to bring troopers down here to help us find these creatures and wipe them out."

A raucous laugh came through the speaker, making Steele cringe. "Yeah, sure," chuckled Moody.

"We can send you the video from the hospital cameras to prove it," Marty interjected. "What's your email address, and we'll shoot it over to you."

"Um, okay," said Captain Moody, with some cynicism. "We'll take a look at it." He gave the email address and Marty wrote it down.

"Awright then," the sheriff affirmed. "We'll get that over to you in a jiffy. Call me back here after you've seen it, then?"

"You got it."

Sheriff Steele hung up and looked at Marty. "You know how to do that video to email stuff?"

Marty nodded. "Sure. It's just a matter of attaching the video file to the email."

"Great. Do it."

The diver proceeded to send an email to the state troopers, and he added the security camera file from the flash drive. Then he sent it to the address Captain Moody had given, and he faced the sheriff.

"There you go," Marty confirmed. "It's on its way. Now we'll just wait a few minutes for them to check it out and call you back."

The men waited anxiously, trying to be patient. Ten minutes went by, and they figured the troopers were watching the video several times to let it sink in. But after twenty minutes, the state boys still had not called back; the sheriff grew concerned.

"Maybe the email didn't get to them," said Steele. "I better call 'em back." He activated the speakerphone and hit redial to call the trooper station again.

"Yes, Jimmy?" said Captain Moody when he picked up, recognizing the number on his caller ID.

"Did you guys get the email?"

"Oh, we got it."

"…And?"

"I've gotta say, Jimmy, that's some great CGI video you guys put together down there. But I'm afraid we're not gonna fall for it."

The sheriff was flabbergasted. "This isn't a fucking *hoax*, Josh! Do you really think I'd waste my time trying to pull *pranks* on you?"

"Um, yeah. But like I said, it looks pretty real. If you put it on YouTube, I'll bet you can get enough hits to supplement your retirement fund."

"Look," said Steele, trying to keep his cool. "I had people killed by whatever the hell these things are, and I need all the help I can get rooting them out and killing them before any more of my civilians get killed."

"If you did have a couple of deaths there, I'm sure you and yours can handle it."

"I'm not fucking around here."

"I'll tell you what," said the trooper. "You just have your Mayor Vargas give us an official call, and then we might take you seriously."

"The mayor's on vacation somewhere on a Mediterranean cruise! Won't be back for a week. That puts me in charge, and I'm giving you the official call. We need your assistance down here!"

"Alright, Jimmy, you've had your fun. Enjoy the rest of your day."

"Fuck you very much." Sheriff Steele picked up the handset and slammed it down, ending the call.

"So I guess we're on our own?" asked Carl.

The sheriff looked his fellow officer in the eye. "Appears that way. Just you, me, and Lewis. But poor old Lewis can't do us much good trying to fight those things. I may have to deputize some more people, like Marty here. Or young Mason Parker, Mr. Criminal-Justice-Degree. If things get out of hand around here, we're gonna need all the manpower we can get."

CHAPTER 24

The sheriff was at the dock, kneeling to untie the police boat from the cleat, when he saw them. Mason, Eaver, and Danny were trotting toward him, their shoes clomping loudly on the planks. They called out to him as they approached. *What now?* he wondered nervously.

He stood to address them. "What's up, kids?"

"My dad's gone missing," said Danny. "Last I saw him was two days ago. I'm afraid he might've been taken by one of those creatures Eaver told me about."

"Hope not," Sheriff Steele said sincerely. "Could be he's just out doin' his own thing. Has he called or anything?"

"No sir, and I can't call him. His phone just goes straight to voicemail. Not that I'm complaining about having some time to myself, but this just isn't like him. I'm a little bit worried."

"I'll add him to the list of people to look for. Turns out young Miss Hannah's gone missing too."

Eaver folded her arms. "Mmm-hmmm," she smirked, knowing the gossip she had heard about Ricky and Hannah was true.

Mason caught Eaver's tone and looked quizzically at her. She merely gave a shake of her head, suggesting he ignore the response.

Danny was too concerned about the sheriff's statement to notice Eaver's reaction. "Hannah's missing too? Hannah Dermont?"

Sheriff Steele nodded. "Yep. Her ma says she hasn't come home in about two days either. So the list is up to Earl Goates, Walt Jr., Sarah Primley, Hannah, and now maybe your dad."

"You going out to look for her on the water?" asked Danny.

"No, son, I'm afraid it's bigger than missing persons. Last night some of those creatures busted into the hospital and killed a few people. Malcolm Gibbs included."

"Oh my God!" said Eaver, her hand involuntarily flying to her mouth.

Mason, stunned, gazed down at the waves lapping the dock moorings. "Mal's dead?" he said without bringing his eyes up. "Jesus."

The sheriff nodded. "So right now, I'm not sure just what to do next. The state troopers won't come down, they think I'm making the whole goddamn story up. My diver thinks their den is somewhere in Pirate's Bend, so I figure I'm gonna take the boat over there to see if I can find any sign of those creatures."

"Something's there in Pirate's Bend, alright," said Danny. "When all of us were there on Sunday we heard some unusual splashing not too far from shore. Sounded like something big. If it was one of those things, it's gotta be living close to that spot."

"Could you tell me exactly where you heard the splashing? That would be a good place for me to start."

"No, not really," said Danny. "But I could show you."

The sheriff winced, reluctant. "I don't know about that. I'd feel better if I didn't have anybody on the boat I'd be responsible for."

Mason offered his input. "I think we should go with you, Sheriff. We can take you right to where the sound came from, and Lord knows the more eyes, ears, and hands you have out there, the better."

The young man had a point. Since Marty had taken the hospital footage home to enhance it and send it to his colleagues to solicit their help, and Deputy Riggins was finishing the unpleasant business of getting hold of the families of those killed in the hospital, the sheriff was alone right now. He was timid about bringing any civilians on the police boat, especially to a potentially dangerous area, but he could use all the assistance he could get right now.

"Okay," he conceded. "But I'm gonna deputize you, temporarily, just to make it official."

"Fine by me," said Mason. "After all, I've got the degree for it."

Danny and Eaver also agreed to the enlistment. The sheriff gave the short and sweet version, officially claiming them as temporary deputies under his jurisdiction. The group raised their right hands, swore to their new duty, and then boarded the cruiser. The sheriff untied the rope from the cleat, flung it inside the boat, and jumped aboard to start the motor.

The patrol cruiser was a twenty-five-foot-long center-console vessel, built strong and unsinkable. Sheriff Steele felt pretty good about the group's safety as long as they stayed on the boat. With a glance at the others and a little nod, he pulled away from the dock.

It was overcast and gloomy, which gave the ocean waves a dull gray hue. The murky water, stirred up by last night's storm, was ornamented with floating seaweed and red algae. The scent of the ocean's viscera was richer than usual as well, but it lightened as the boat cruised farther away from shore.

While the vessel traveled across the water, Mason found himself studying Eaver from the corner of his eye. He admired her bravery and companionship. Despite the crazy events of the last twenty-four hours, she would not be scared off; she was still right here in the thick of it. She had always been a steady, loyal friend to have. He watched her while the wind blew her highlighted hair back, exposing her face and neckline, and he could not help thinking how lovely she had become over the years. She had indeed blossomed into an attractive young woman.

It only took ten minutes for the vessel to arrive at the mouth of Pirate's Bend. The sheriff turned the wheel, steered into the cove, and reduced speed.

"Okay, kids," he said, "eyes and ears sharp. I still can't wrap my head around what we're up against, but if it's in here I want you all to stay alert and well inside the vessel."

"You got it," Mason affirmed. "After seeing one of these things up close, I'm on full alert here."

"Ditto," said Eaver, her back pressed safely into her chair and her hands firmly holding on to the armrests.

The patrol cruiser sputtered along the surface of the cove, its occupants scanning the surrounding water fervently for any signs of animal life.

As they reached the center, Danny nudged the sheriff. "It was right around there," he said, pointing. "That's where we heard the noise in the water."

Sheriff Steele followed the young man's finger to a spot not more than fifteen feet from shore, near a notch in the rocky shoreline. "Okay," he acknowledged. "Let's cruise over there." He steered the patrol boat toward the notch.

When they got to the spot, the sheriff cut the engine. The boat slowed to a crawl, quietly coasting while the waves slapped against the hull. The group surveyed the surrounding water for any sign of the beasts they were looking for, but the sea offered none. After twenty minutes, they agreed it was time to try searching somewhere else.

Steele started the motor and cranked the wheel left to turn away from there. Just as the boat started pulling away, Mason saw a dark-green, snake-like object burst from the water and strike the transom, hooking into the boat's edge with a white talon.

He instantly recognized the dark thing as a tentacle from one of the monsters.

"Sheriff! Sheriff!" he cried out. Another tentacle latched onto the transom, and the creature began to climb up the starboard corner of the stern.

The sheriff looked back to see what Mason was hollering about. When he saw the monster trying to pull itself aboard, his heart skipped a beat. "Jesus," he muttered, actually seeing one of these things with his own eyes. He immediately grabbed the gun on his hip.

Mason's eyes darted, looking for something to use as defense against the aggressive creature. He saw an aluminum paddle stowed next to him in the boat's sidewall, and he quickly reached for it. He swung the paddle desperately at the animal in an attempt to keep it at bay.

A gunshot went off, and Mason saw the creature's body take the hit. The sheriff's shot winged it between two tentacles, shredding tissue and spraying blood. The beast convulsed, retracting its tentacles, and fell backwards into the water.

Their hearts pounding, everybody watched the edge of the stern earnestly while the vessel moved forward. With any luck the bullet had injured the animal enough to send it fleeing back into the depths. But then they saw a tentacle whipping over the transom and digging in. The creature began to pull itself out of the water again.

Eaver screamed. *"It's still alive! Go, go, go!"*

Sheriff Steele pushed the throttle all the way, hoping to shake the monster from his boat. But the willful animal held strong and continued its attempt to board the vessel.

Danny couldn't move. He wanted to, but he was paralyzed with shock. He was frozen in his chair, his legs pulled up against his chest, white-knuckled hands gripping the seat.

Mason jammed the paddle against the hostile creature's body and pushed with all the strength he could muster. Then Mason noticed the submerged tentacles on its left side were dangerously close to the boat propellers.

"Turn right! Turn right!" he yelled.

The sheriff pulled the wheel to the right, and the outboard motor swung that way. A tentacle fell into the whirling propeller and became wrapped in it. The creature was yanked down and pulled toward the blades. Its tangled tentacle was ripped free from its body, but by then it was too late. The propeller had already found the monster's midsection and was chopping it up vigorously. Blood and tissue was churned into the water.

"Yeah!" Mason exclaimed, the exultation of triumph overtaking his fear. He leaned over the stern, thrust the paddle at the distressed creature, and pushed it further against the strong propeller. It took no time at all for the blades to render the beast dead.

The sheriff, his heart still pounding wildly, cut off the engine and rushed back to look at the carcass. "Jesus Mother Mary," he uttered.

The tattered body sank into the depths, slowly drifting out of sight. All that remained on the surface were shredded chunks floating in a stew of blood, and the air was thick with the smell of sulfur and fishy flesh.

"God, that's a stink," Danny remarked.

Mason looked at the red carnage littering the water. Then he turned his head to Eaver. "Like crab cakes," he said with a slight grin. "All you need now is some ketchup."

Eaver hurried to the edge of the boat and threw up.

CHAPTER 25

They wasted no time getting out of Pirate's Bend. Having narrowly escaped the attack of just one creature, the sheriff realized they were not equipped to be out there with however many more that may be lurking in the waters. But at least now he could confirm that the monsters were in that area of the cove.

Danny had barely spoken a word since the frightening encounter, still in shock. Eaver was quiet too, her arm locked tightly around Mason's. They just gazed out at the water as the boat made its way back to the dock.

After tying the patrol boat to the moorings, the sheriff ushered the others off the vessel and onto the wooden dock. Then, seeing his cruiser still parked near the beach, he led his young partners ashore.

Steele stopped and turned to face them. Now that they were safely on land and no longer in danger, his mind was free to consider their emotional well-being. "Are you all okay?" he asked.

Mason looked at Eaver, who nodded. Then he said, "We are, thank God. But that was a harrowing experience."

The sheriff studied Mason, sizing him up. "You did good out there, son."

Mason shrugged. "Did what I had to, I guess. Although next time we go on an expedition, you better give me a gun."

Sheriff Steele grinned. "It's a deal... deputy. You know how to handle a gun?"

"Yessir."

"Then, if there *is* a next time, I'll hook you up." Steele then shook his head nervously. "But I'll be damned if I go back out there unless I absolutely have to. I'm gonna see if my marine biologist might have a better idea for taking care of those things."

Mason wanted to be involved for the duration of this ordeal. "Mind if we tag along?" he asked.

The sheriff nodded. "I've got no problem with that." The young adults would definitely not be in the way, and might even be able to offer helpful suggestions. At this point, the more assistance he had the better.

Danny, however, had other plans. "Sorry, but I need to get home," he stated. "Just in case my dad shows up, or if he tries to call the house."

"Alright, buddy," said Mason. "We'll give you a call if we find out anything about your dad." He slapped Danny's shoulder, and then watched him turn and walk away.

Sheriff Steele brought Mason and Eaver to his police cruiser and let them inside. Then he started the vehicle, dialed Marty Bennett's phone, and drove toward the station.

Half an hour later, Marty arrived at the police station to join them. After having heard the sheriff's account of what happened, he was eager to help engineer a plan for dealing with the mysterious creatures.

He entered the building, seeing the others gathered at the front desk. Sheriff Steele was on the radio, telling Carl to come in. When the sheriff was finished with that, Marty spoke to him.

"So just what the hell happened out there?" the diver asked. "Did you really kill one?"

The sheriff nodded. "We did. I got a shot off and winged it, but ol' Mason here is the one who killed it. He pushed it into the propeller, which chopped it up into pieces. It was nasty."

"I believe it," said Marty. "Were they as horrible as they looked on video?"

"Worse." Steele closed his eyes tightly. "Looked like something from Hell had a threesome with something from the ocean and something from outer space."

The diver remembered the security footage images vividly. "I still can't believe it. It's one thing to try to fathom their existence after watching the video, but now hearing that you saw one up close... wow."

"And I never want to see one again. But at least now we've confirmed they're in the cove, and what area they're in."

Marty arched his eyebrows. "Right by Pirate's Point, huh?"

"Yep. We were attacked in the water real close to there."

"Well, that clinches it. That cavern I found beneath Pirate's

Point has to be their nest. So now all we have to do is go kill them."

"You got any ideas how?" asked Mason.

The diver nodded. "Um-hmm. I think some well-placed underwater explosives would do the trick."

Sheriff Steele was intrigued. "How do you mean?"

"Well," said Marty, "I'll plant the explosives at the mouth to the cavern and blast it shut. The creatures will either be blown up or be trapped inside. Either way, they'd die."

"*You* want to plant the explosives?" the sheriff asked.

"Yes, and immediately. We need to jump on this while we still have daylight. I have the gear at my house, shouldn't take me long to get it all together and get back in the water."

A shiver ran down Steele's spine. "I think that's a bad idea, Marty. You don't want to be in the water with those things. We had enough trouble with one of them trying to climb aboard the boat!"

"Sheriff, I'm sure it'll be fine. I've been down there before, and this time I'll bring weapons."

"Marty! There could be a *dozen* of those things swimming around there for all we know!"

The diver shook his head. "I don't think so. I think the one you encountered was a rogue anomaly. These things are clearly nocturnal predators, and probably won't come out of that cavern until nightfall."

"I don't know..."

"Trust me, Sheriff. We go in now, while the sun's still up, and take care of this before they have a chance to come out again tonight."

The sheriff looked to Mason for input, and Mason shrugged. "I think he's right, Sheriff. If we don't do this now, there could be more deaths tonight."

"Okay. Just be damn careful when you're down there, Marty. Dr. Warden told me those things have poison in their claws."

"Alright, then." Marty stood and dug for his keys. "I'm going home to load up all the gear I'll need."

"Alright," Sheriff Steele acknowledged.

"I'll meet you at the cove in an hour," Marty stated. "Then we'll seal that cavern up so they starve and die."

CHAPTER 26

Marty pulled into his driveway and parked the van. Then he hurried inside the house to gather his supplies. He could not afford to waste any time getting back to the waters of Pirate's Bend – the more daylight he would have while underwater the better.

He moved through the house and headed for the shed in the back yard. Swinging the door open, he went to the workbench inside. Marty pulled his Mares Sten Mini speargun from the wall and a handful of stainless steel shafts armed with double-barbed tips. Then he went back into the house for the rest of his gear.

The diver collected his mask wetsuit from the utility tub in his laundry room. Next he turned to his air compressor station and grabbed two full air tanks. He brought them out to the van, and then went back into the house for the final necessary items.

Heading to his guest bedroom, which was difficult to navigate because of all the accumulated clutter, he made his way to the footlocker in the closet. He yanked the wool blanket that was covering it, then opened the lid. Inside he found his stash of explosives. He took out half a dozen sticks of dynamite and a spool of detonator cord, then stuffed them in a backpack and returned to the van. Armed with all he would need, Marty left his house and drove back to Pirate's Bend.

By the time the sheriff had gotten Carl caught up, left him to man the station, and arrived at the cove with Mason and Eaver, he saw Marty's brown van coming around the opposite bend. He parked the cruiser, stepped outside, and stood to face the oncoming van.

Marty stopped his vehicle and set the emergency brake. Then he got out and waved for the others to join him. While the group came closer, the diver opened the side panel and prepared to load up with gear.

"You got everything you need?" asked Steele, still leery about this excursion.

Marty nodded while stripping down to his underwear. Mason and Eaver politely turned away while the diver slipped into his wetsuit. But Marty thought nothing of changing in front of others; just another day at the office for him.

"Okay, help me take some of this down to the water, will ya?" said Marty, standing in his neoprene outfit.

The sheriff took the flippers and air tank Marty handed to him. Then he watched while Marty turned back to the van and pulled out the backpack containing the gelatinized dynamite and detonating material. "I take it that's the explosives," said Steele.

"Yep," the diver replied. "Good old dynamite."

Eaver, curious, craned her neck to see inside the backpack. "I've never seen real dynamite before." It looked just like she imagined.

"What the hell do you even keep something like that for?" Sheriff Steele asked.

"Well, you know, for blasting stumps or clearing boulders and such."

"You have a lot of need for that?" the sheriff smirked.

Marty hesitated before responding. "Okay, you got me. I like blowing shit up. Sometimes I bring some up to the cabin when I'm shooting and stuff. Sue me."

"Where did you even – you know what, I don't even give a shit," said Steele, throwing a hand up. The only thing that mattered right now was the success of this marine operation. "As long as you know how to use it."

"Here, son," said Marty, handing the speargun and shafts to Mason. "You all take this stuff for me, and I'll carry the explosives down."

Sheriff Steele looked at the 20-inch weapon with skepticism. "Is that little speargun powerful enough to protect you from those things down there?"

"It may not kill what we're dealing with, but it'll sure hurt enough to send 'em away." Marty was not sure if his statement was true, but the speargun was better than nothing. "Besides," he admitted, "it's the best I've got."

"Well Jesus, Marty," said Steele, "just be careful down there."

Marty gave an acknowledging salute. "Should be easy enough. I'll place the explosives at the mouth of the cavern, get away, and blow it. Simple as that."

"Are you sure that's the only entrance?" Steele asked.

"Pretty sure. That was the only entrance into the pool, and the cave walls were all solid everywhere else in the chamber. Plus it was the only way out when I got spooked and fled out of there last time. So yeah, sealing this will do the trick."

"I sure hope so," added Eaver. She knew that if the creatures could get out, more people were likely to get killed.

Marty secured the speargun to his side by strapping it into its modified leg holster. Then, making sure he had a few extra barbed shafts tucked next to the weapon, he picked up the backpack of explosives. He put it on backwards, wearing it in front.

"Do me a favor," said Marty. "Someone click this tight around my back."

Mason stepped closer, helped the diver position the shoulder straps, and then fastened the clasp. "Okay," he said, "you're secure."

Marty gave the backpack a slight tug to check. "Thanks." Then he donned his air tank and mask. The diver walked into the water, turned to give a final thumbs-up, and disappeared beneath the surface.

The water was murky, greenish-brown. But the sunlight penetrated well enough to where he could effectively see his surroundings. He wished he had an M1 underwater gun for this dive. The six-round waterproof gun would have been a comfort to have, but he did not own one. At least he had his speargun; and it was a decent one. Marty was about as safe as he could be in this water. He kicked forward, heading for the corner of the cove where the underwater cave was.

He found the mouth of the cave and paused to turn on his flashlight. Then, after a quick feel inside the backpack to make sure the dynamite and fuse was with him, he proceeded into the dark cave.

After twenty feet of confinement, he reached the section that broadened into a more spacious chamber. *This might be a good spot to blast*, he thought. *But further in would be better*. He continued his swim through the limestone passageway.

While swimming, he felt a sudden change in the water current next to him. His skin crawled as he realized something could have just swum past him in the black water.

Marty quickly aimed the flashlight behind him.

Nothing but floating sediment and zooplankton dancing in the light beam.

Just creeping myself out, he reasoned. *Focus on the job at hand, set up the dynamite, and get the hell out of here.* He kept moving forward.

Sixty feet in, he was now at the opening to the large cavern containing the egg pool. This was the spot. After a final sweep around him with the flashlight to make sure Marty was still alone in the water, he carefully pulled the explosives out of his pack. He positioned them around the base of the rocky opening, strung on detonator cord. Satisfied at his placement of the dynamite, he unrolled the rest of the detonator cord. Then he began swimming back toward the cove with the unraveled wire in hand.

On his way, he couldn't shake the creepy feeling that something was going to attack him before he made it out of the water. He kept the flashlight aimed forward and his hand holding the wire close to the Mares Sten on his hip. His heart was pounding anxiously.

Finally the diver arrived at the mouth of the cave. The light coming from the cove outside was a warm welcome, inviting him safely out. Marty emerged from the underwater cave and took cover against the adjacent rocks. Then, still gripping the detonator cord, he pulled the detonator from the backpack. He enabled it, took a deep breath, and activated the trigger.

The dynamite exploded deep inside the cave, sending shock waves out through the rock and water. Marty felt the force rumble through his body. It made his nerves tingle.

On the road, the others heard the muffled blast. Their eyes grew big with awe and hope. Then, when they saw Marty's head breach the surface, they cheered. Marty heard the response and acknowledged the people on shore with a wave and a thumbs-up. The mission was a success; the monsters were trapped inside their lair to die. Victorious, the diver smiled and swam back to the road to join his elated partners.

CHAPTER 27

Sheriff Steele uncapped the bottle and began pouring into the paper cups. The aroma of Johnnie Walker Black floated across the sheriff's desk and into the noses of all. Marty and the sheriff smiled in anticipation.

Eaver held up a hand in polite refusal. "None for me, thanks," she stated.

The sheriff shrugged. "More for us, then." He handed cups to Marty and Mason, and then raised his own to toast. "Here's to killing monsters."

"Here here," said Mason. He took a small sip of the whiskey, absorbing the flavors slowly.

Marty shot his down in one long swallow. "Ahhh... I earned that one."

"Hell, you've earned another," said the sheriff. He refilled Marty's cup. "That was a job well done today, sir. Well done."

Eaver nudged Mason. "And I think we've earned dinner. Wanna go see Momma at the restaurant?"

Mason nodded. "Yeah, I could go for some food." He finished his whiskey and set the cup on the sheriff's desk. "You guys mind if we cut out on you?"

"Not at all," said Steele. "You two go and enjoy. It's been one hell of a day. Get on outta here. And thank you for all your help today."

"You're welcome, Sheriff," Mason replied. "See you fellas later." He gave a departing handshake to the sheriff and Marty. Then he and Eaver left Sheriff Steele's office and headed outside.

The sun was dissolving into the horizon, decorating the sky with vibrant pinks and oranges. Eaver admired the sunset with a quiet, thankful smile. She wrapped her arm inside Mason's and they walked the streets to Sherrie's Shack.

The couple arrived at the restaurant and walked inside. There they saw Sherrie and Cinch polishing tables. Sherrie set down the cloth and went to her daughter to give her a hug.

"There you are," Sherrie sighed. "I'm glad you're back. I was wondering where you two were."

"You probably wouldn't believe us if we told you," said Eaver.

"Try me, sweetie."

"Well, we went out to Pirate's Bend on the sheriff's boat to find where the monsters are coming from, one of them attacked the boat, and we killed it."

Cinch's eyes popped wide. "De sligger? You killed de bogeyman o' de water?"

"We did."

"Do you have de body?"

Mason shook his head. "Oh no. The propeller chopped it up pretty good. It's fish food now."

Sherrie seemed less surprised than Eaver expected. "I still don't know what to think about all this monster talk, but I don't want you out on the water again. Will you do that for your momma?"

Eaver held her mother's hands. "Don't you worry, Momma. It's not a problem anymore. Mr. Bennett went to their cave underwater and blew it up with dynamite. It was really cool, you should've been there."

Cinch drew closer, intrigued by the news. "He blew dem up?"

"Trapped 'em in their nest to die," Mason clarified. "Whatever survived the blast will starve to death."

"So we're safe now, Momma," said Eaver. "No more monsters will be breaking into here again."

"Aww, you mean I brought that ol' thing here from the house for nothing?" said Sherrie sarcastically, tilting her head toward a shotgun leaning in the corner by the kitchen.

"Well, not necessarily... you might get rude customers," Mason said in jest.

"Or Mal's buddies," added Eaver, less jokingly.

Sherrie raised an eyebrow. "Touché."

"The restaurant looks good," noted Mason. "A lot better than it was this morning." The broken window had been covered with plastic sheeting stapled to the frame, the blood and broken wood were cleaned up, and the gouges in the wall had even been spackled over.

"We've been busy. Even had a pretty decent lunch rush, just had to keep that side blocked off." Sherrie smiled. "You two hungry? How about I whip up some sandwiches for us all?"

"Please," Eaver and Mason said in unison.

Sherrie and Eaver went to the kitchen and began putting sandwiches together. Cinch reheated his soup and pulled four bowls down for the group. Before long they were enjoying a simple but satisfying dinner.

While they ate, Cinch prodded for more information about the creatures. "So you saw de sliggers; what did you think when you saw dem?"

Mason leaned back. "Oh my God. I was like 'what the hell is *that?*' – I couldn't believe my eyes. Yesterday you said *you* saw one?"

"Yes," said Cinch. "By my house de other night, when I be fishin'. It was dark, but I know what I saw. Came right for me. I ran home fast as I could."

"Jesus," muttered Eaver. "And we didn't believe you. I'm sorry, Cinch."

The old Creole shrugged. "A hard thing to believe. I'm just glad you don't think me crazy anymore."

Eaver gave the cook a hug. "Oh, Cinch… we still think you're crazy."

Everybody at the table laughed. The mood was relaxed, friendly. The group continued their pleasant meal together.

Right about when they were finished, the bell above the door jingled. The group noticed the entering patrons, and quickly got up from the table to welcome them inside. Sherrie sat her guests and brought them menus. Then she returned to her group.

"Why don't you two go find something nice to do?" she proposed.

Eaver looked at Mason. "Whatcha wanna do?"

"I'm beat," Mason confessed. "Let's just go to my house. We can put on a movie and relax on the couch."

Eaver found the idea appealing. "Sounds good. You sure you don't want us to stick around and help, Momma?"

"I'm sure," Sherrie smiled. "Cinch and I can handle it here."

CHAPTER 28

It was half an hour after sundown when the sheriff got the call. He was taking a quiet, peaceful drive on the back roads around town to unwind from the whirlwind of the long day. The calm of the dirt roads at night was working, until Carl's voice blurted for him on the two-way radio.

"Whatcha got, Spud?" asked the sheriff, somewhat disappointed by the interruption to his tranquil drive.

"Mrs. Johnson called, says she heard a commotion next door at ol' Ms. Murphy's house. Like someone was breaking in through a window."

"Kimberly? On Silas Hill?"

"Yeah. You near there?"

Steele unknowingly nodded. "Near enough. I'll be there in five minutes."

"Ten-four. Over and out."

"Out." The sheriff set the microphone on the cradle. Sighing, he steered his cruiser toward town.

A few minutes later he was at Silas Hill Road, which overlooked the adjacent coast. He parked the car and stepped out, hearing the waves in the dark from beyond the trees. Then, knowing which house was Kimberly Murphy's, he grabbed his flashlight and walked toward the house.

As he neared the front porch, he saw that all the lights were off and one of the windows was smashed in. Crouching down just a little, he pulled his gun and continued his approach.

The front door was unlocked. He opened it and announced his presence. "Ms. Murphy? Sheriff's Department. Are you in here?"

There was no reply. Steele scanned the dark room, noticing upturned furniture and broken glass on the floor.

And a sulfuric odor.

The sheriff's heart rate quickened, the stench triggering his memory of the deadly sea creatures. "Ms. Murphy? This is Sheriff

Steele." He stepped through the front room and moved toward the kitchen. "Ms. Murphy?"

When he entered the kitchen, he saw a body lying on the linoleum floor. The beam from his flashlight confirmed it was the body of Kimberly Murphy. She had been savagely attacked and killed, blood covering her ripped and bitten body.

"Sweet Jesus..." muttered the sheriff. He spent a moment mourning the loss of a sweet old lady, then realized the killer could still be there. His eyes hardening, he gripped the gun tightly and began searching the rest of the house.

Whatever had killed her was gone now. After making sure the house was clear, Sheriff Steele returned to the street outside. He looked all around for any movement or signs of the creatures. Nothing out there with him.

Noticing the lights of the other houses on the street, he decided he had better warn them about what had happened. He knocked on each door, explaining to the residents that the area was not safe and that they needed to lock themselves inside their homes.

Once the neighbors were informed, the sheriff returned to his vehicle, reached for the two-way, and called in to his deputy.

"Hey Spud, you there?"

Carl's voice crackled back through the speaker. "Affirmative, chief."

"Listen, we got us a problem. Ms. Murphy's dead. Looks like she was killed by one of those goddamn sea monsters."

"What?"

"See if you can call Lewis into the station so you can help me patrol and look for 'em."

"Um, okay. What if I can't get hold of him?"

"Then I guess nobody will be at the station for a while. I need your eyes and ammo out here."

"Ten-four."

Sheriff Steele then headed for his cruiser. He would pick up Carl, but on the way he needed to stop at his own house to make sure his family was okay. He started the engine and sped home.

The image of Ms. Murphy's mutilated body stirred panic in him. If those things had gotten inside *his* house and attacked *his* loved ones... he would be lost if anything happened to them. He pressed heavier on the accelerator.

When he arrived at his home, everything looked normal. The door and front windows were intact, and the usual lights were on inside. He relaxed a little. Parking the cruiser, he shut the engine off and hurried inside the house.

"Betty?" he called when he opened the front door.

"Hey, baby," his wife replied from the kitchen. She popped her head out, brown hair pulled back into a ponytail. "Are you finally home for the night?"

Steele shook his head. "No, hon. Afraid not. Are the boys home?"

"Yeah, they're both watching TV," she said, walking toward him.

"Good."

Betty detected urgency in her husband's eyes. "Jimmy, what's going on?"

"I'll just come out and say it. There are monsters, sea animals, that have been killing people the last few days. We thought we trapped them in their cave today, but apparently they found a way out. I just found Ms. Murphy dead in her home."

Betty's hand flew to her mouth. "Oh no! Kimberly?"

"Killed by those things. They're roaming around and breaking in through windows. I need you to lock up the house behind me, take the boys upstairs, and secure yourselves in our room. Make sure you have the gun ready up there. Just in case."

"Jimmy... you're scaring me."

"You'll be fine," he reassured, although he still had his fears about losing them. "Just batten down and keep the gun in hand. I've gotta go get Spud and look for those things. I'll call you to check in."

The sheriff then went to the living room to instruct his boys to do exactly what their mother told them, that he would be back as soon as he could, and that he loved them. After a parting kiss to his wife, he left the house and started the police cruiser.

CHAPTER 29

Reverend Jenkins stood silently at the pulpit, staring out over the empty pews. He hoped for inspiration. Although the next service was three days away, the reverend was anxious to begin writing his sermon for Sunday. He just needed to decide what the weekly topic would be.

There were the usual themes, like peace, love, faith, and hope. Or he could shake it up a bit by speaking about spiritual growth, forgiveness, wisdom, or Satan. Ultimately he would like the topic to be relevant to events that had occurred over the week.

Imagining his congregation before him, it was easy to determine what would benefit them the most on Sunday. He could picture the face of Lena Dermont, and the worry over her missing daughter. He could picture the families of the people killed at the hospital. There would be loss and sorrow in their eyes, despair. They would need a strong message of hope and faith.

Reverend Jenkins had his direction. He would quote from Romans, Corinthians, Matthew, and John. Now inspired, the reverend left the pulpit. He started walking toward his office to sit and write.

Something struck one of the stained glass windows. The loud smack caused the reverend to jump and spontaneously put his hand on his chest. *A tree branch*, he mused. *Couldn't be anything else.* He fixed his eyes on the colorful panel of Jesus and the angels.

Another blow against the glass, this time sending cracks across the stained glass.

An intruder? But why? Why would someone break into a church?

A third strike of the window finished the job, shattering it inward. Tiny fragments of colored glass reflected the light of the votive candles they flew past. The shimmering spray was pretty. But what came next was not.

The reverend's eyes widened in horror as he watched something hideous entering the church through the demolished window. His mind could not comprehend what he was seeing – his muscles froze.

Serpent-like appendages pulled forth a monstrous creature. The huge, black eyes were maddening to look at. It had terrible teeth, like long needles, in its jutting snout. Its large, shiny body slipped quickly through the window frame. The creature was like nothing that existed in this world – perhaps it was a demon from the underworld. It even *smelled* like Hell.

Then another appeared, following the first one inside. The reverend's panic grew, and his pounding heart beat even faster.

The beasts moved fluidly along the wall, their tentacles working with their strong hind legs to maintain their balance. They spotted Reverend Jenkins; one of them circled to block the main entrance while the other charged straight for him. The aggressive, almost angry, hissing sound that emanated from its gaping jaws made the reverend's skin crawl.

Realizing it would be upon him in seconds, he broke his frozen stance and turned to run between the pews. His leg caught the corner of a bench, affecting his footing as he tried to run. The reverend fell to the floor.

The beast was right on top of him. Reverend Jenkins looked up to see the creature raise a tentacle and lash it down toward him. He cringed, instinctively rolling his body beneath a pew. The sound of something sharp penetrating wood followed. The reverend opened his eyes to see a white claw stuck in the wooden seat above his face.

Adrenaline surging through him, the reverend wriggled his body until he was in the next row of pews. Then he got to his feet and ran. The second creature was still blocking his path to the main entrance, so he hurried to his office on the side wall.

Reverend Jenkins made it to his office, slamming the door shut behind him. He locked it, wondering if the monsters could even turn doorknobs. Probably not, but they would just break the door down instead. He knew he only had a few moments before they would get to him. The reverend's eyes darted around the room to look for an answer.

He noticed the attic ladder door, tucked tightly into the ceiling. *Aha!* he thought. *That's the answer.* He quickly reached for the rope handle and yanked the attic ladder open. Then he scampered up the ladder as he heard violent pounding at the door. The reverend made it to the attic and hurriedly pulled the ladder shut with shaking hands.

As soon as he was hidden in the darkness he heard the door give in the room below. He could hear the beasts rampage through his office, heaving and breaking and smashing. But they would not find him there.

Reverend Jenkins closed his eyes and silently prayed that God would get him through this night.

CHAPTER 30

"Let's go, Spud."

"Affirmative," Carl acknowledged, slipping into the passenger seat. He strapped on his seatbelt while the sheriff drove away from the station.

"I can't believe they got out," said Sheriff Steele, with tiny shakes of his head. "It's those *things* that killed Ms. Murphy, Spud. Same types of wounds, and they left that rotten egg smell behind."

The deputy was in shock – he was terrified by the idea of going up against the monsters he saw on the hospital video. "Jesus, boss. You sure you and me can handle 'em?"

"Got that right. They can be killed, just like any other animal." He patted the Smith & Wesson sidearm on his hip. "And we've got the firepower to do it."

"I hope so."

"Besides, we're the law. We've gotta protect the town from these killers."

Carl's resolve stiffened. "Damn straight, Sheriff."

"Now keep your eyes open. They could be anywhere."

The deputy activated the spotlight mounted on the passenger side and began shining it around the houses they patrolled past. The light beam danced around the yards, illuminating mailboxes, trees, bushes, and porch furniture. For ten minutes they roamed but saw nothing out of the ordinary.

Then Carl caught something in the spotlight. His heart jumped nervously as he thought he saw something dark and shiny dart behind the corner of a house. "Jesusjesus, I think I just saw one!"

Steele stopped the car. "Where?"

"Right over there, just went behind Joe Reynolds's house," whispered Carl.

"Okay, let's go." The sheriff parked the cruiser and opened the door. He stepped out, drawing his flashlight and gun. "C'mon, Spud."

Carl's fear of confronting these monsters still pumped through his body. He wanted no part of this. But he knew that was not an option. He had sworn to be a police officer, to serve and protect his town and community. It was time to man up.

The deputy got out of the vehicle and joined his boss. "Right with you, Sheriff."

The two quietly hastened through the front yard and around to the side of the house. The sheriff paused in the dark corridor, holding Carl back with him. He shined his flashlight in every direction to make sure nothing was waiting to ambush them. Seeing the area was clear, he and the deputy continued their search.

When they reached the back yard, they noticed the glass patio door was broken through.

Steele led his partner onto the patio and to the rear doorway. Slowly, cautiously, they entered the house.

The kitchen light was on, and the sheriff could see more light coming from the front room ahead. "Sheriff's Department!" he announced loudly. "Anybody home?"

There was no answer. He called out again, and again received no reply. This was eerily familiar, just like when he found Ms. Murphy dead in her home earlier. And the same sulfuric scent was in the air. He raised his pistol, ready for anything.

The officers proceeded to the front room. They saw broken end tables, glass and wood fragments scattered across the floor. Then they spotted the body lying face down on the carpet. The victim's shirt was shredded, as was the tissue beneath. A great deal of blood had flowed out from the deep gashes to create a dark pool around the body.

"Shit..." Carl muttered. "That looks like Joe."

"Poor bastard." Steele looked closer, recognizing the profile of the bloody head as that of Joe Reynolds. Then the sheriff placed his fingers on the victim's neck, feeling for a pulse. He shook his head. "He's dead. Body's still warm though. Whatever did this might still be in the house."

They carefully searched the rest of the house. After checking every room, it was clear the killer was gone now. The men exited the house and paused in the front yard to look around.

"So what next?" asked Carl. "Do we call the ambulance?"

The sheriff thought hard. "Not just yet. I don't want to bring people out here while those things are loose."

"Makes sense."

"We gotta find these things, Spud. Kill 'em before they kill more people."

CHAPTER 31

"Goodnight, now," waved Sherrie with a grin. Her diners bid her the same and exited the restaurant. Sherrie looked up at the wall clock. It was almost nine.

Cinch popped his head out from the kitchen. "Dat de last of dem?" he asked.

"That's it," said Sherrie. "Time to close 'er down." She walked to the door, locked it, and flipped the sign from OPEN to CLOSED. Then she went to the counter to bring out the cleaning supplies.

Cinch starting washing the grill while Sherrie wiped down the dining room tables. He conversed with her while they cleaned both rooms. "I'm glad we got de place fixed up in time for customers today."

"Me too," Sherrie replied. "It broke my heart when I saw it all tore up last night. We did a lot of work today, but I'm glad we did. It feels like a restaurant again." She craned her neck toward the kitchen. "I'm gonna have to give you another raise, Cinch. You're my lifesaver."

The old Creole smiled. "You are family, Sherry, you know dat. But of course I'll take more money from you. My granny didn't raise no fool."

"This the same granny that told you about the – " She paused to remember the name. " – 'sliggers'?"

"Yes, ma'am. Just like her mama told her."

Sherrie stopped working and stood straight, hands on hips. "So your family has been telling each other about 'bogeymen of the water' for as far back as that?"

"Yes. Lots of de Creole know about de sliggers."

"Well, I have to admit, I have no other explanation for what the kids say happened in here last night. But I still can't believe that they really saw what they say they saw." Sherrie shrugged. "I dunno." She resumed her wiping.

When she had finished with the dining room, she brought her handful of cleaning supplies to the counter. That was when she heard the loud sound of something hitting the plastic sheeting covering the broken window. She whipped her head around toward the window.

Cinch heard it too, and appeared from around the corner. "What was dat?" he asked, concerned.

Sherrie shook her head. "Not sure." She took a step into the dining area to get a closer look.

The plastic was struck again, this time the resounding impact ripping it loose from the duct tape around the window. Sherrie jumped. While the black plastic floated down to the floor, tentacles reached inside and pulled a massive body in through the missing window.

"*De sligger! De sligger!*" Cinch shrieked. He disappeared into the kitchen.

Sherrie's mind could barely process the sight before her. The creatures Mason and her daughter told her about were real. *And here*. She stood frozen, her eyes fixated on the monstrous creature.

The thing locked its horrible black eyes with hers. It opened its wide snout and hissed loudly, viscous spittle spraying from its teeth. The beast reared up on its reptilian legs, pushed off with its thick tail, and rushed toward Sherrie.

With a scream of terror, Sherrie broke her paralysis. She turned and lunged for the kitchen, instinctively diving behind the counter. *Great*, she thought, instantly regretting her decision, *now I'm cornered.*

She saw Cinch appear from the kitchen, this time with his cleaver in hand. There was just a hint of fire in his eyes. The old Creole had returned for battle – he would not stand idly by while his beloved Sherrie was in danger.

"Get away!" he commanded to the monster that was almost upon him.

The creature stopped. Just for a second, though, to size up the new prey. Then it continued its charge.

Cinch hurled the cleaver. It hit home in the creature's midsection, and the cook could hear his blade slipping into the moist flesh. The beast's six tentacles flailed in a frenzy of pain. One of the appendages struck the counter next to Cinch.

Sherrie saw the milky claw dig into the edge of the counter. Then she noticed something below the claw, leaning against the inside of the counter.

The shotgun she had brought from home.

Quickly she reached for the weapon and pulled the pump back. Then she leapt to her feet to come to Cinch's aid. Seeing the creature up close made her heart skip a beat, but that did not prevent her from doing what she had to. She aimed the shotgun, pressed the stock against her shoulder, and pulled the trigger.

The blast disintegrated the monster's head. Pieces of dark green and pink sprayed across the dining room, covering the tables with juicy tissue. What remained of the beast fell backward onto the floor.

The smell of rotten eggs was stronger than ever now, and Sherrie fought the urge to vomit. She grabbed the box of shotgun shells that she had also set behind the counter. Then, tentatively, she walked into the dining room to prepare for any more potential intruders. Cinch followed her.

They sat at the table with the least gore. Keeping the gun aimed at the open window frame, Sherrie waited diligently for another monster. After ten minutes, she began to think there would not be another attacker.

Relaxing a little, she set the shotgun and box of shells on the table. Then, after another five minutes of quiet processing, she felt the urge to find Eaver.

She turned to Cinch. "Let's get out of here."

The Creole shook his head, his eyes fearfully wide. "No, ma'am. I'm not going out dere. Best we stay in here where we can see 'em comin'."

Sherrie frowned, wanting to be with her daughter. But then Cinch's logic appealed to her; outside they would be more vulnerable. At least in the restaurant they had light and the monsters were walled out. "Alright," she surrendered, pulling the box of shells closer. "We'll batten down here for a while."

CHAPTER 32

"Need another beer?" Eaver called out from the kitchen.

Mason checked his, noting it was almost empty. "Sure."

Eaver returned to the front living room with two bottles of beer and sat down next to him on the couch. "Okay. Now we're ready."

Mason aimed the remote at the DVD player and pressed play. They had watched Finding Nemo about twenty times together over the years, but it was still a sentimental favorite. And it would be the perfect escape from reality that they needed tonight. The two nestled into the couch as the animated movie played.

Half an hour later, Mason thought he heard a noise at his front door.

He looked at Eaver. "Did you hear that?"

She shook her head. "Huh-uh."

Mason pressed the pause button and craned his neck toward the door. He heard a slight scratching of the wood, along with a muffled cry.

"Sounds like a cat," said Eaver. "Do the neighbors have one that comes 'round?"

"No. But you're right, it does sound like a cat." He stood up and walked to the door.

Mason hesitated. For just a second he feared it could be something else on the other side of the door. Something monstrous. But he shook the fear off, realizing they had taken care of that nightmare. He turned the knob and opened the door.

Sure enough, he found a tabby pacing at the door. The feline waltzed right into the house. "Yep. It's a cat, alright."

Eaver saw it as it pranced into the living room. She immediately recognized the tan coat with black and gray striping. "Captain Purrbucket! What are you doing over here?" She looked at Mason. "It's Cappy, Hannah's cat. Should we take him back there?"

Mason shrugged. "If anybody's there. Maybe we should call first to see."

Eaver agreed. "Yeah, and I'd like to know if Hannah's still missing. Okay, gimme a minute." She pulled out her phone and called Hannah's house.

After six rings, Eaver frowned.

"No one there?" asked Mason.

"Huh-uh. Nobody's picking up. Maybe her momma's out looking for her. Bless her heart." She ended the call, then opened her contacts list to see who else she could call about finding the cat. Then her screen notified her that her battery was drained and the display faded. "Okay, now my phone's dead."

"No biggie, you can charge it tomorrow."

Eaver turned her attention to their furry visitor. "How long have you been stuck outside, Cappy? I'll bet you're thirsty." She addressed Mason. "Can I give him a bowl of water?"

"Sure, bowls are up in the cupboard by the fridge."

She walked to the kitchen, the tabby at her heels. Finding a bowl and filling it with cold water, she set it on the kitchen floor and gave the cat a quick scratch behind the ear. Cappy responded with a purr and began drinking. Then Eaver made her way back to the couch. Mason resumed their movie.

Minutes later the cat joined them in the front room. Cappy paced the room, familiarizing himself to his surroundings. Then, as if something caught his attention, he suddenly scurried to the front window.

Cappy reared his back and hissed, his fur bristling.

"What's wrong with him?" Eaver said curiously.

Mason frowned. "Must've seen something he doesn't like. Or heard, or smelled. Raccoon or possum, I suppose."

The cat was growling now. His eyes were locked on the window.

Eaver got up. "C'mon, Cappy, that's enough. Whatever's out there is probably bigger'n you anyway." She walked to where the tabby was perched and bent down to pick him up.

The window busted inward, shattering. Eaver fell backward to the floor. The cat jumped from her arms and dashed out of sight. Mason sprang from the couch to see what had happened.

One of the sea creatures was coming in through the window frame, slick and shiny.

"No! No way!" cried Mason. *How the hell did they get out?* He was sure they would never see these monsters again after Marty had sealed the entrance to their cavern. Mason hurried to get Eaver out of harm's way.

Eaver had rolled away from the window and was scuttling across the floor toward him. *"Jesus! Mason!"* She reached up, and he pulled her to her feet.

The beast was standing in the room, and now Mason could see a second creature making its way through the window.

Mason's eyes darted around the room, desperate for some kind of weapon. Nothing but furniture. Mason grabbed a lamp, yanking it free from the outlet. Backing away from their unwanted visitors, Mason pushed Eaver slowly into the main floor hallway.

The monster raised its appendages and hissed loudly. Then it charged toward its human quarry.Mason and Eaver ran.

They immediately heard the smashing of the back door and realized another beast was breaking into the kitchen. They stopped in the middle of the hallway.

"Shit!" said Eaver. "Whatdowedo, whatdowedo?"

"The stairs! We gotta get upstairs before they trap us!" They turned around to hurry back, seeing the first beast was already at the end of the hallway.

Mason hurled the lamp at the attacker, and it cracked against the beast's head. The blow was enough to daze it, stopping it in its tracks. The split second was enough to allow Mason and Eaver to cut around the stairway and scamper up the steps.

Upon reaching the second floor, Mason led Eaver down the narrow hallway and to his bedroom. They rushed inside and locked the bedroom door behind them. But they knew it would not take long for the persistent creatures to find them.

"Now what?" Eaver asked, panicked.

Mason looked around. There were no items in the room that could be used as a viable weapon. He glanced at the bedroom window, and realized that would have to be their escape plan.

"C'mon! Out the window!" Mason opened the window. Peering outside, he stepped through onto the mild pitch of the roof. He pulled Eaver through to join him, then closed the window again. They stepped aside, away from the window, to be out of sight from the bedroom. Then Mason looked down to find a good place to descend.

He pulled Eaver tightly against him and held a hand to her mouth.

Eaver spotted them too. Three more of the monsters had gathered in the front lawn below. Mason did well to cover her mouth – otherwise she might have screamed when she saw them.

Luckily the beasts in the yard had not yet noticed the couple on the roof. Mason slowly, gently, sat down with Eaver on the shingles. They lay back against the roof to keep out of sight.

The creatures inside broke through the bedroom door. Mason and Eaver could hear the commotion while the beasts searched the room for their prey. Violent smashing, breaking, and knocking things around.

Eaver had never been so frightened. Her heart was pounding so hard that she could hear her own rapid pulse. "What do we do?" she whispered, as quietly as she could.

"I don't know," Mason whispered back nervously. "We gotta stay right here, and not move."

The two kept perfectly still on the roof, huddled together. All they could do was wait and pray that the beasts would not come out onto the roof.

CHAPTER 33

"Over there!"

The deputy followed the sheriff's finger, aiming the mounted spotlight in that direction. The bright beam found a shattered window on the front of a lightless house. "The window?"

"Yeah, I just saw something go in there," the sheriff stated. He put the vehicle in park and shut off the engine.

"Ms. Surrow's house," noted Carl. "I think she's out of town."

"C'mon, Spud." Sheriff Steele opened the door and sprang from the car. Pulling his sidearm and pointing it up in the air, he hurried through the lawn and up the steps to the front porch. Carl was right on his heels.

The smell of sulfur was in the air. With a quick glance to his deputy to make sure he was ready, the sheriff opened the door and quickly stepped back. The door swung inward, revealing nothing but the dark.

"Be ready," warned Steele.

"You got it," Carl assured.

The sheriff aimed his flashlight into the house, holding it beneath his gun hand. The men tentatively entered Ms. Surrow's home, prepared for the monster to appear at any given moment.

"Ms. Surrow?" called the sheriff, just in case she was home. After no answer, he figured Carl was right about the kindergarten teacher being out of town.

The lights came on in the entryway, illuminating the hallway and front room. Surprised, Steele jumped a little. He turned to see the deputy's hand on the light switch. He chuckled. "Yeah, I guess that would help."

"Um, yeah," Carl smirked. "Light good. Dark bad." He closed the front door and followed the sheriff further inside.

They slowly approached the kitchen. The sulfuric odor grew stronger. Steele tightened his grip on the handgun – the beast was close. When the men arrived at the kitchen entrance, the sheriff reached for the light switch on the wall. He found it and flipped the light on.

A large creature was standing in the middle of the kitchen. Its horrific features were fully visible in the fluorescent light, and Carl shuddered at the sight of the monster before them. The shiny, dark-green skinned creature was a hundred times more terrifying up close than it was in the hospital footage.

It reared back, hissed aggressively, and lashed out with two of its barbed tentacles.

"Look out!" exclaimed the sheriff. The men jumped back, away from the appendages that struck the linoleum floor just in front of them. Then Steele took aim and fired repeatedly, planting nine slugs into the monster's midsection and head. Carl added five more from his weapon. The 9mm hollow points effectively ended the life of the attacking beast. It collapsed to the floor, oozing.

All was silent in the kitchen. The officers stood frozen, weapons still aimed at the monster, the air around them smelling of gunpowder and rotten eggs. Carl merely stared at the thing, his mind still processing what had just happened.

"Yeah!" the sheriff barked triumphantly, breaking the moment of silence. "*That's* how you do it!"

The deputy snapped back to who he was, what he just shot, and why they were there to do it. "Yessir, that's one monster that won't be hurting anybody in *our* town."

"C'mon, Spud, let's make sure there aren't any others in here." The sheriff moved toward the next room, and the deputy was at his side.

They continued their search of the main floor and found nothing. Their sweep ended on the second floor, which was also devoid of any other monsters. Satisfied, they casually walked back down the stairs.

"Now what do we do?" asked Carl. "I mean, with Ms Murphy's body, and Joe Reynolds, and the body of this thing in here."

"We can probably call the ambulance out now," said the sheriff. "But I still don't think the town's safe yet. I want to keep searching to make sure there aren't more of them out and about."

The deputy nodded in agreement. "Works for me."

They arrived at the front door, and Carl reached for the doorknob. Just then he heard something on the other side of the door, like something rubbing against the wood, and he stayed his hand.

"Did you hear that?" he whispered, eyes wide.

Steele nodded slowly. "I did." The sheriff raised his gun and took a step back. He took a deep breath. "Open it."

Carl turned the knob and briskly pulled the door open. To their amazement, the men saw four more monstrous creatures in the doorway. When the beasts spotted the men, they hissed and charged into the house together.

"Shit!" Steele yelled. He and Carl instinctively retreated while shooting at their attackers. The beasts were taking hits, but were still advancing.

After six shots, the sheriff was empty. Reacting quickly, he ejected the clip and replaced it with his spare. He chambered the first round and continued firing at the onslaught.

"I'm out!" cried Carl, absolute fear in his voice.

Steele remained focused on killing the attackers. He aimed at their weaving heads, landing a couple of good kill shots. Two of the four fell dead, and the others were badly wounded. But they were still coming.

Then the sheriff was out of bullets.

"Ahhhh, shit!" he said. "I'm out too." He knew their only hope was to get out of the house. "C'mon, Spud! We gotta make a run for it!"

Sheriff Steele ran toward the remaining creatures to get past them and to the front door. Carl was right behind him. The beasts grabbed the officers attempting to flee, digging their talons deep into them. The men screamed in pain and dread. They felt the cold tentacles squeeze tightly around their bodies, the barbed tips stabbing them, and then the agonizing sensation of the monsters' sharp teeth tearing away chunks of flesh. The deputy caught sight of the sheriff while one of the creatures took a bite from his boss's throat that silenced the sheriff's shrieking.

Carl pounded at his own attacker, fists beating wildly against the beast's snout and razor-like teeth. Finally he was able to wriggle free from his weakening captor. He pulled himself to his feet, lumbered away, and glanced back to see the wounded beasts finally succumbing to their bleeding bullet wounds. The deputy was bleeding a lot himself, and he was aware of his dire situation. He staggered through the front door and onto the dark porch. Then he toppled down the steps and landed flat in the grass.

Carl looked out across the lawn, seeing the sidewalk, the street, and the houses beyond with nervous people peeking out their windows. Summoning all his strength, he began crawling toward them. But he was losing too much blood. The deputy lost consciousness before he could make it to the concrete sidewalk.

CHAPTER 34

The sun had been up for just a little while. Mason acknowledged the light through his eyelids, but kept his eyes closed to rest them. He still had Eaver under his arm. Feeling her body stir, he opened his eyes.

They were still on the roof, lying uncomfortably on the shingles. He needed sleep. Eaver slept a little, but Mason had tried to stay alert throughout the night just in case the beasts returned to the property. Perhaps he had gotten some brief moments of slumber during the night hours, but if he did it was minimal.

Eaver sat up quickly and surveyed the yard below them. Seeing that the monsters were gone, she relaxed her back muscles and exhaled. Then, feeling the stiffness from lying on the roof, she stretched her arms over her head.

"It looks like they were never here," she said, still gazing at the lawn.

Mason nodded. Just the familiar green centipedegrass around the house and the chirping of birds in the surrounding trees. "Yep. Like it was all just a nightmare." He slowly sat up. "Come on, let's get back inside."

"What if some of 'em are still in there?"

"Naw. It looked like they all left together, and I never saw any of 'em come back."

Eaver was satisfied. "Okay. Let's go in."

They cautiously got to their feet, established their balance on the slight incline, and made their way back to the bedroom window. Mason peered inside to make sure the coast was clear. It was. He entered, followed by Eaver.

The first thing they noticed was the lingering smell of sulfur in the room. Then they took in the sight of scratched and cracked furniture and the shredded mattress on the bed. Everything in the room had been overturned or moved.

"God," said Mason. "They really did a number on this room. Must've wanted us pretty bad. I guess we're lucky they didn't look for us outside."

Eaver had a creepy feeling. "You sure you saw all of 'em leave?"

"Yeah, I'm sure. Plus I don't think they could stay out of the water for this long. And they don't like the daylight anyway." He put his arm around her shoulder. "C'mon."

They moved through the narrow hallway and down the stairs to the main floor. Mason stopped at the bottom of the steps. His heart sank when he saw the carnage.

The front room was ruined. The couch was ripped up, the antique furniture was shattered, the pictures were smashed, and everything was littered with a shiny, clear residue trail. Everything in the room that brought cherished memories to Mason was now destroyed.

"My house," he mourned. "I can't believe it."

Eaver rested a hand on his shoulder. "I'm so sorry, sugar."

Mason was pissed. "Fuck these things," he seethed through his teeth. "I'm gonna kill them all."

"We'll get it fixed up," Eaver reassured, trying to calm him. "You'll see."

"Maybe, but some of this stuff was irreplaceable." He drew his gaze to what used to be the front room window. "I wonder how many other houses they attacked last night."

Eaver's eyes widened as she suddenly thought about her mother. "I gotta call Momma." She pulled her phone from her pocket, then frowned when the black screen reminded her that the battery had died.

"My phone's dead. I need to check in with Momma."

Mason agreed. "Let's get over to your house."

Just then they heard a car pull up in front of the house and stop abruptly. They looked through the broken window to see Sherrie get out of the car and trot toward the house.

"Momma!" shouted Eaver. She opened the door and ran outside to greet her mother, and Mason followed.

"Oh baby," Sherrie grinned, tears welling at the sight of her daughter. "Thank God you're here. I've been trying to call you. Are you okay?"

"Yeah," said Eaver, hugging her mother. "But you wouldn't believe the night we had."

"Those monsters you told me about?"

"Uh-huh. Broke into the house and almost got us. We had to spend the night up on the roof."

"Oh baby," Sherrie said again. "One came into the restaurant last night. Blew its brains out with the shotgun."

Mason stepped closer to the women. "We've got to get over to the police station. Find out what they're gonna do about this."

Eaver nodded. "Yeah, I wanna know what we're supposed to do next. And find out if anyone got hurt last night."

Sherrie was also curious to hear how the police would respond to this, but her filthy, contaminated restaurant was a deeper concern. "I'm gonna go back to the restaurant, to help Cinch clean up the nasty mess and do more repairs. But get in, I'll drop you two at the police station."

They filed into Sherrie's car and Sherrie drove them away from the house. While traveling the streets, they noticed quite a few other houses with broken windows, either on front porches or above trampled bushes. Last night's activity was more substantial than they had thought.

Sherrie arrived at the police station to find all the parking spaces in front of the building already occupied. She stopped her car in the middle of the street to let her passengers out. Then, after kissing her daughter, she waved and drove off to join Cinch back at the restaurant.

Mason and Eaver entered the station and saw about twenty townspeople crowded inside. Danny was among the group, and he acknowledged his arriving friends with a nod. The sheriff's family was there also, and they were crying woefully. Mason had a bad feeling.

Deputy Lewis Simkins was at the desk, looking older than his fifty-eight years this morning. Marty was standing next to him, and together they were trying to console and reassure the shocked community. Mason and Eaver wedged through the group and joined Lewis and Marty at the desk.

"Glad you two are okay," said Marty. "Looks like we didn't do as good a job as we thought yesterday."

"Those things got out, alright," Mason avowed. "They

attacked us in my house last night. And several other houses, judging by what I saw on the way over here."

"Yeah," Marty affirmed. "They came out with a vengeance, apparently. Reports of them attacking all over the coastal side of town. Killed several people."

"Where's the sheriff?" asked Eaver.

"He's dead. They found what was left of his body inside Ms. Surrow's house last night, and Spud on the lawn."

"Oh my God…"

Mason was afraid to ask. "And Spud?"

Marty shook his head. "He died early this morning in the hospital. Toxins in his blood."

"Poison from the claws?"

"Yep. I'm pretty sure."

Mason turned to Deputy Simkins. "Well we have to call the state police again," he said. "They *have* to come help after this."

Lewis nodded. "I did. They said they could get troopers to us by tomorrow."

"*Tomorrow?*" scoffed Marty. "And let those things come back out tonight? We could lose half the town before tomorrow. We've got to take care of this today."

"How?" the old deputy asked. "I'm the only police here now."

Mason raised a finger. "Not necessarily. I was deputized yesterday. So technically, you're not alone."

"And I might as well be considered a deputy," added Marty, "as many times as I've helped out the sheriff over the years."

The pudgy old deputy nodded, appreciating their enlistment. "Okay. First thing I think we should do is evacuate the town," said the deputy. "But some won't leave; they either have no place to go, no means to get there, or just won't want to leave."

Mason thought for a moment. "I guess you could set up cots in the high school gymnasium. Anybody who wants to stay in town would be safe inside. It's all brick walls and steel doors – nothing could break into there tonight."

"Alright, but that still leaves the problem of what to do about the creatures."

Marty straightened his back. "We just have to finish the job we thought we'd done yesterday. The explosives I planted underwater were done right; that entrance is definitely sealed. The only other opening to their cave was the hole at the top. You know, the fenced-off one on top of Pirate's Point. So we'll just have to go down through there and seal them up for good."

Mason was on board. "Count me in."

Marty turned to Mason. "I won't lie; I could use all the help I can get. But are you sure you want to put yourself in that kind of danger?"

"Yeah," Mason replied. "If we don't wipe them out now, they'll just come back out tonight and I'll be in danger anyway."

"You have any rock climbing experience?"

"Are you kidding?" said Eaver, recalling her memories of Mason's cliff scaling. "Captain Spelunker here? Yes, he can climb."

Marty was satisfied. "Alright, then. Let's get on it. We need to finish the job while it's low tide." He eyed Mason gravely. "Once we get down there, I can't guarantee we'll make it out. Are you sure you want to help me with this?"

Mason glimpsed around the room, noting the solemn faces of those who lost loved ones last night. He knew the feeling all too well, having recently lost his own mother, and he hated watching others suffer the same pain. He returned his attention to Marty.

Mason's face was stone. "Mr. Bennett, I want nothing more than to kill these fuckers."

CHAPTER 35

The group approached the hole atop Pirate's Point. They walked slowly, guns ready in case they saw any of the monsters emerge from the cavern beneath. But the hole was dormant. It almost seemed smug, daring.

Mason held the late sheriff's Smith & Wesson in one hand, keeping the 9mm handgun aimed at the dark opening, and was carrying a plastic gas container in the other. Marty was at his side with a second gas container and one of the shotguns from the police station. They stopped when they were about ten feet away, just outside the broken rope fencing that used to surround the hazardous hole.

Eaver set down the duffel bag of explosives they had picked up at Marty's house. She looked at the two men while unloading the coil of rope from her shoulder. "You guys sure you wanna do this?"

"Of course not," Marty said, a cheesy smile on his lips. "I'm scared to death right now. But it's gotta be done."

"How about we just dump the gasoline down there and burn 'em all up?" Mason suggested.

Marty shook his head. "I considered that, but it would be a short burn. The creatures would probably duck into the pool and stay underwater until it burned out... they'd survive."

"Then let's just drop the dynamite down there with the gas."

"Wouldn't do the trick. The explosion would just be concussive. The dynamite needs to actually be placed in the walls to effectively blast them down."

Mason shrugged. "I guess we're goin' down, then."

"We're goin' down," Marty confirmed. Then he grabbed one end of the rope and brought it to the nearest tree. He secured the nylon rope around the tree using the sturdiest knot he knew, and then doubled it. If this knot failed, they wouldn't make it back.

Mason kept his weapon pointed at the hole. He watched Marty pull the rope tight and unroll the rest of it. Marty then weaved the loose end of the rope through the handles of the gas containers, laying the containers on the ground near the hole. Next he fed the sixty feet of remaining rope down the hole. The diver looked at Mason and nodded; he apparently had a plan of attack.

"Alright," said Marty. "I'll go first, with the explosives. You follow right after and cover us." He turned to Eaver. "Then, when we are safely on the ground, we'll call up and you push the gas cans down the line. One at a time."

Eaver drew a deep breath to calm her nerves. "Okay, I'll be ready."

"Weapons check," Mason advised. He made sure the 9mm Smith & Wesson was loaded, the safety was off, and that he had his extra fifteen-round clip of hollow points. "I'm good."

Marty pumped the twelve-gauge, loading one of the eight shells from the magazine tube. "Me too." He tugged on his gloves to tighten them around his hands. After slinging the shotgun and duffel bag around his elbows, he gripped the rope and stepped to the rocky opening.

"Don't forget," Marty warned, "stay clear of those tentacles. Their claws are poisonous."

"I'll remember."

Marty lowered himself into the hole.

This was it. Mason hurried to stay right behind him. He sat down at the opening and placed the top of the gun barrel in his teeth to temporarily free both hands. He locked eyes with Eaver for a bittersweet second, each seeing true affection in the eyes of the other. Then he reached down, grabbed the taut rope, and descended.

Clamping the rope with his feet, Mason took one hand off the line to remove the gun from his teeth. He rested a finger on the trigger and continued down, his eyes following Marty's flashlight beam as it illuminated the cavern.

The hollow was breathtaking. About forty feet in height, it was a glorious haven adorned with massive calcium stalactites, sparkling walls, and white stalagmites reaching up from the floor. It would be soothing if not for the lingering stench of sulfur reminding the men of the danger lurking therein.

The air was stagnant. No breezes could effectively enter the hole to cycle fresh air through the chamber. As a result it was uncomfortably warm, muggy, and pungent in the cavern.

Marty's hand was beginning to cramp. He would maintain his cautious rate of descent, however, to make sure he did not rush to the bottom before knowing the coast was clear. Seeing no forms of life in the flashlight beam, he continued dropping until his feet were on the rocky floor.

He stepped aside to let Mason finish his descent, pulling the shotgun into a ready position. His eyes were already adjusting to the dark environment. But he kept the flashlight on to see as well as they possibly could. Mason got his feet on the ground and readied his weapon as well.

They heard water moving, like something slipping in or out of the pool. Marty whipped his flashlight toward the sound and saw what he knew they would. Two of the cavern's inhabitants appeared from the water to fend off the intruders. They charged from the pool with a frenzy of splashing.

Marty pulled the trigger, blasting one of them in the midsection with double-aught buckshot. The lead balls destroyed the target, which flew backwards into the water. Mason, fighting to control his shaking, squeezed off several rounds at the second beast. One of the hollow-point bullets found a sweet spot in the head. The creature fell dead.

All was calm again. The men's ears were ringing, loud enough to drown the sound of their hearts pounding.

"Are you okay?" Eaver called down nervously.

"Yeah!" Mason announced, keeping his eyes on the water. "We're good!"

They continued to watch the surface of the pool to make sure no other sentries were coming. After a few minutes, they deemed themselves safe for the moment.

"Alright," said Marty, "send down the first gas can!"

Eaver dragged the plastic container along the rope and to the hole. Then she pushed it in, and the container slid rapidly down the line.

Marty caught the gas and pulled it free from the rope. "Now the other one!" He watched the second container drop down the rope, and he corralled it as well. He turned to Mason. "Okay, cover me while I get started with the explosive."

Mason nodded, relieving his partner of the shotgun. He was quite aware that there were many of the monsters in the cavern with them, at least as many as he had seen last night. They would show themselves at some point. He needed to keep a keen eye on their surroundings.

Marty wasted no time. He pulled a handful of dynamite from the duffel bag and walked across the flowstone floor to start placing the explosives in the walls. He set four-stick bundles into rocky crevices at each location, crimping the bundled safety fuses to the blasting caps. Within minutes he had covered the cavern with four blast zones.

A splash in the water sent a jolt through Mason. He locked in on that spot in the pool, but saw nothing but ripples.

Marty saved the last bundle of dynamite for the egg pool. He approached the six-foot-wide hollow in the rock and looked down. Sure enough, there were the objects he remembered seeing. Dozens of greenish-yellow orbs, the size of footballs, submerged in the crater. Reaching over the crater, he wedged the explosive into a perfectly-sized gorge in the rock wall.

"Explosives placed," the diver confirmed. "Now gimme the gas."

Mason picked up one of the gas containers and handed it to Marty, all the while maintaining his eye and gun hand on the dark water.

Marty started pouring gasoline in strategic areas, away from where the burning fuses would be. He soaked the corners, splashed parts of the wall, then emptied the container into the egg pool.

"That's good enough," Marty stated. "Otherwise we risk the gas catching before we get out."

"What about the other gas can?"

"Hand it over, I'll set it by one of the explosives. For extra oomph."

Mason handed his partner the second container. Marty set it on the lip of the egg pool crater, just below the dynamite. Next he began laying the fuse out, walking backwards while straightening it. Then he looked at Mason.

"Alright, now. Ready to go? As soon as I light these we go back up the rope."

Mason nodded. "Ready. How much time will we have to get out of here?"

Marty studied the five fuses, each boasting a length of ten feet. "Plenty. About five minutes."

Another splash was heard, and again Mason's flashlight darted to the source to see only ripples. He was sure they were being watched from underwater. He could imagine a dozen creatures hiding beneath the surface, just waiting for the men to try to leave. It gave him chills.

"Here we go," said Marty. He pulled a lighter from his pocket and lit the first fuse. As soon as it started to crackle, he hurried to the next fuse. He lit them in succession, made sure they were all burning, and then joined Mason's side.

Mason handed Marty his shotgun back. "Let's go, chief," the young deputy said.

Just then the water erupted. Five slithering monsters surfaced, their appendages flailing wildly as they attacked. The men took aim and began shooting to hold them back.

One of the thrashing tentacles sliced Marty's hand. The cut was deep, painful. His fingers instinctively flew open, causing him to drop the shotgun.

"Fuck!" the diver exclaimed. He knew immediately that he had been poisoned by the creature's toxic claw.

"Marty!" shouted Mason. He continued firing at the beasts to allow Marty time to retrieve his weapon. Marty's hand darted down and picked the shotgun up.

Two of the beasts had fallen, succumbing to Mason's lethal gunshots. But before Mason could kill any more, one of the monsters struck Mason's gun hand with the side of its tentacle. It did not scratch him, but the blow knocked his pistol away. Mason heard the gut-wrenching splash as the gun disappeared into the pool.

Marty blew another beast away with the shotgun. "Get up the rope!" he yelled, pushing his partner away.

Mason had no weapon, so he could no longer fight. He went for the rope, almost tripping over the calcium stumps on the floor.

Marty kept shooting at the remaining attackers. Another claw landed, digging into Marty's calf. It yanked him off his feet. He kept the shotgun in his grasp, and continued blasting away at the monsters. One of them got awfully close just before a shell turned its head into mist.

Within seconds the beasts surrounding Marty were dead. He was extremely thankful for that, since he knew he was about out of ammo.

Then another four surfaced from the pool.

"Come on!" said Mason.

Marty shook his head. "Go up! I've gotta keep 'em off you."

"You have to come with me!"

"I can't," Marty declared. "If we both go, they'll take us down before we get high enough!" He glanced down at his bleeding hand, the wound already itching. "Besides," he added, "I've been stung – I'm gonna die no matter what. Now hurry!"

"Marty…"

"Go!"

Mason obeyed, knowing the diver was right. He took one last look at his partner, then at the fizzling fuses. Taking a focusing breath, Mason grabbed the rope and began climbing.

The next wave of creatures rose from the water and charged toward the men. Marty pumped the shotgun and fired his remaining two shells. Gritting his teeth, he flung his empty weapon angrily at the remaining attackers. Then he roared a battle cry and lunged at one of the creatures. He tackled it, pushing it backward. The rest of them converged, pulling the huddle into the water.

The rope felt slick through Mason's gloves. He had only made it up several feet, and was already having trouble keeping his grip. He took a quick look to the thrashing water, seeing the creatures tear into Marty. The diver's maddened screams ended.

The beasts now turned their attention to Mason, spotting him on the rope. They emitted loud, hostile hisses that curdled his blood. Then they rushed from the water and toward the dangling prey.

A jolt of adrenaline surged through Mason, and his body tensed. He squeezed the rope as hard as he could and climbed desperately. By the time the monsters arrived below him, he was ten feet off the ground. He continued to ascend until he had to stop for a breather. Looking up, he could see Eaver looking down through the opening above.

"C'mon, Mason!" she urged.

The rope began moving beneath him. His eyes darted down to see the creatures wrapping their appendages around the rope and yanking on it. He prayed they did not figure out how to climb.

It was now or never. Mason pulled with all his might. He had to ignore the numbing of his muscles – all that mattered was getting out of there. Twenty-five feet off the ground. Then thirty.

He wondered how much time was left before the fuses ignited the dynamite. The concept of time had vanished when the creatures began their attack. Did he still have enough time to make it? His heart raced at the thought of the explosives going off any second.

"C'mon!" Eaver repeated, more urgently.

Mason kept pulling, his strength ebbing. Thirty-five feet. Thirty-seven. Thirty-nine.

Then, when he had nothing left, Eaver reached down and grabbed his arms. She pulled hard. The assistance was enough to help Mason get to the top of the opening. His feet finally able to make contact with the ceiling rock, he used his legs to push himself the rest of the way through the opening.

Eaver pulled him out of the hole, falling backwards with him. Mason was grateful to finally be above ground again. But they were not out of danger yet.

"Move it, Eaver, it's gonna blow!"

The couple scampered to their feet and ran like hell. They were not twenty feet away from the hole when they heard and felt the explosives detonate.

The blasts were thunderous, deafening. Mason and Eaver almost fell to the ground, but stayed on their feet. They kept running as the earth rumbled beneath their feet. As they ran, they turned to look at the site behind them.

The surface of Pirate's Point collapsed, dropping into a heap of rocks, smoke, and dust. Mason and Eaver, a safe distance away, stopped and gazed at the transformed landscape. The entire area now rested twenty feet lower than before. Eaver stared in awe, then turned her head to Mason.

Eaver broke, tears beginning to flow from her eyes. "I've never been so happy to see you," she said, her voice quivering. She chuckled at how frail she sounded.

Mason felt the same way about seeing her. Without thought, he placed his hands around her face and delivered a long, gentle kiss to her lips. She did not tense up or recoil, but rather kissed him back with equal enthusiasm. It felt right.

When they separated, Mason smiled. "It's gonna be okay now," he vowed. She nodded and he embraced her.

The air still smelled of gunpowder mixed with the stink of sulfur. A part of Eaver wondered if it was really over. She chose to ignore that unsettling thought and held Mason tighter. Surely he was right; it was going to be okay.

Eaver looked out, beyond the rocks, and gazed into the calm of the rolling ocean.

CHECK OUT OTHER GREAT DEEP SEA THRILLERS

THEY RISE
by **Hunter Shea**

Some call them ghost sharks, the oldest and strangest looking creatures in the sea.

Marine biologist Brad Whitley has studied chimaera fish all his life. He thought he knew everything about them. He was wrong. Warming ocean temperatures free legions of prehistoric chimaera fish from their methane ice suspended animation. Now, in a corner of the Bermuda Triangle, the ocean waters run red. The 400 million year old massive killing machines know no mercy, destroying everything in their path. It will take Whitley, his climatologist ex-wife and the entire US Navy to stop them in the bloodiest battle ever seen on the high seas.

SERPENTINE
by **Barry Napier**

Clarkton Lake is a picturesque vacation spot located in rural Virginia, great for fishing, skiing, and wasting summer days away.

But this summer, something is different. When butchered bodies are discovered in the water and along the muddy banks of Clarkton Lake, what starts out as a typical summer on the lake quickly turns into a nightmare.

This summer, something new lives in the lake...something that was born in the darkest depths of the ocean and accidentally brought to these typically peaceful waters.

It's getting bigger, it's getting smarter...and it's always hungry.

CHECK OUT OTHER GREAT DEEP SEA THRILLERS

MEGATOOTH
by Viktor Zarkov

When the death rate of sperm whales rises dramatically, a well-respected environmental activist puts together a ragtag team to hit the high seas to investigate the matter. They suspect that the deaths are due to poachers and they are all driven by a need for justice.

Elsewhere, an experimental government vessel is enhancing deep sea mining equipment. They see one of these dead whales up close and personal...and are fairly certain that it wasn't poachers that killed it.

Both of these teams are about to discover that poachers are the least of their worries. There is something hunting the whales...

Something big
Something prehistoric.
Something terrifying.
MEGATOOTH!

BLOOD CRUISE
by Jake Bible

Ben Clow's plans are set. Drop off kids, pick up girlfriend, head to the marina, and hop on best friend's cruiser for a weekend of fun at sea. But Ben's happy plans are about to be changed by a tentacled horror that lurks beneath the waves.

International crime lords! Deep cover black ops agents! A ravenous, bloodsucking monster! A storm of evil and danger conspire to turn Ben Clow's vacation from a fun ocean getaway into a nightmare of a Blood Cruise!

 SEVERED**PRESS**

CHECK OUT OTHER GREAT DEEP SEA THRILLERS

PREHISTORIC BEASTS AND WHERE TO FIGHT THEM
by Hugo Navikov

IN THE DEPTHS, SOMETHING WAITS ...

Acclaimed film director Jake Bentneus pilots a custom submersible to the bottom of Challenger Deep in the Pacific, the deepest point of any ocean of Earth. But something lurks at the hot hydrothermal vents, a creature—a dinosaur—too big to exist.

Gigadon.

It not only exists, but it follows him, hungrily, back to the surface. Later, a barely living Bentneus offers a $1 billion prize to anyone who can find and kill the monster. His best bet is renowned ichthyopaleontologist Sean Muir, who had predicted adapted dinosaurs lived at the bottom of the ocean.

MEGALODON: APEX PREDATOR
by S.J. Larsson

English adventurer Sir Jeffery Mallory charters a ship for a top secret expedition to Antarctica. What starts out as a search and capture mission soon turns into a terrifying fight for survival as the crew come face to face with the fiercest ocean predator to have ever existed- Carcharodon Megalodon. Alone and with no hope of rescue the crew will need all their resources if they are to survive not only a 60 foot shark but also the harsh Antarctic conditions. Megalodon: Apex Predator is a deep-sea adventure filled with action, twists and savage prehistoric sharks.

www.ingramcontent.com/pod-product-compliance
Lightning Source LLC
Chambersburg PA
CBHW051945170626
46808CB00007B/2487